Chemical Bonds

ISBN # 978-1-78651-337-3

©Copyright L.M. Somerton 2016

Cover Art by Posh Gosh ©Copyright 2016

Interior text design by Claire Siemaszkiewicz

Pride Publishing

## Books by L.M. Somerton

*Tales from The Edge*

Reaching the Edge
Living on the Edge
Dancing on the Edge
A Double-Edged Sword
Rough Around the Edges
Scorched Edges

*Investigating Love*

Rasputin's Kiss
Evil's Embrace
Tarot's Touch

*The Wyverns*

Mantrap
Deathtrap
Rattrap

*Warlocks*

Elemental Love

*Sexy Snax*

Black Dog

*What's His Passion?*

Testing Lysander
Picturing Lysander

*Anthologies*

Hard Riders
Racing Hearts
His Rules

*Single Titles*

The Portrait
Mountain Rescue
Stroke Rate
Chemical Bonds
Tagging Mackenzie

# CHEMICAL BONDS

## L.M. SOMERTON

# Dedication

To exploring your boundaries.

# Chapter One

Max Allenby pedaled like the hounds of hell were after him. He was late for work. Again. Sharp-fanged puppies from Hades had nothing on his boss—the woman was the devil in disguise and her pitchfork was always firmly aimed at Max's behind. It was an absolute certainty that she was going to rip him a new one. He cursed the nail that had speared his front tire. He had no idea how long his temporary patch would hold but at least he had enough common sense to carry a repair kit. He gave himself a mental pat on the back. His mom always fondly accused him of being 'all brains and no common sense' and now he'd proved her wrong. The victory didn't make up for the fact that his ass was grass if he didn't speed up.

He flew round corners with scant regard for his safety, bent low over the handlebars. Plymouth, New Hampshire was not the busiest town in the world but it was still reckless to ride so fast in bad weather. Rain stung his face and the wind whipped his collar-length hair into his eyes. Somehow the stuff always managed to escape his helmet however much he attempted to confine it. The leather pack that contained his work clothes banged against his spine as he hurtled over the ridges in the road. They were designed to slow down drivers on the approach to Armacom's security gates, but Max didn't have time to reduce his speed. Through strands of wet hair, he could just make out Zeb the security guard sheltering in the gatehouse. Max applied his unreliable breaks and skidded to a dramatic halt about an inch from the barrier, back wheel sliding to the side.

"Hey, Zeb!" Max pulled the lanyard from beneath his

T-shirt and waved his pass at the bemused guard. "Wet enough for you? Could be time for that move to Florida."

Zeb grunted. "Late again, Max? Dr. Preston's gonna have your hide this time."

"Make that every time. I got a stupid puncture. Had to stop and repair it." Max panted his explanation and waited for the barrier to rise. "Don't tell Justin, okay?"

"He might be your big brother, but he's my boss and I like a quiet life. Your secret is safe with me." Zeb grinned and raised a hand as Max accelerated away toward the low, white building in the distance.

Fortunately for Max the bike racks were a lot closer to the building than the staff parking lot at Armacom. It was one of the very few advantages of using an environmentally friendly mode of transport. On a day like today, when he was wet, tired and miserable, convenient parking wasn't much compensation. He was entirely focused on calculating just how late he was going to be by the time he had locked up his bike, run to the changing rooms, made himself respectable instead of the soggy, sweating mess he was at that moment, and reached the lab. *Too long. Way, way too long. I am gonna be in shit so deep I may never resurface.* His boss had a number of subtle and creative ways of making him suffer and he wasn't looking forward to facing her one little bit.

He didn't bother to dismount and wheel his bike toward the racks—he kept cycling and aimed his front wheel for the metal channel that would hold it in place. It wasn't the safest approach but it might shave a few more seconds from his tardiness. The next thing he knew he was sailing through the air while his bike, the laws of momentum in full swing, crashed into the racks. *So man can fly, after all. This could be my big scientific discovery. Why has nobody else identified this latest step in the evolutionary tale yet?* He hit the ground hard and rolled to a halt with a pained moan. Because being airborne didn't last, that was why, and landing was painful.

8

Max remained on the floor while he tried to make sense of what had happened. The ground was a mass of puddles but as his clothes were already sodden he dismissed it as irrelevant. He detected the low purr of an engine idling nearby. A car door opened, then closed with an expensive-sounding thunk. Footsteps approached, then two feet clad in inordinately shiny shoes stopped next to his head. Max couldn't help but compare them to his own scuffed sneakers. It was about time he invested in a new pair but he was allergic to the mall and there were much more stimulating activities to get involved with online than shopping. He must have banged his head — it was full of nonsense.

"You're making the pavement very messy. Get up, boy."

The voice issuing the order was hard and commanding. Max's heart beat faster. Deep growly voices never failed to get him interested.

"Not a boy," he grumbled. He executed a clumsy roll onto his back and squinted at the owner of the shiny shoes and the sexy voice. When he realized who they belonged to his stomach flipped over and it wasn't a pleasant sensation. His day couldn't get any worse. Then he realized it was a possibility — he could still get fired. The command to get up was one he could live with. Concrete was not a comfortable surface to lie on. In a series of uncoordinated movements, he managed to get to a kneeling position. Apparently nothing was broken because movement didn't elicit shrieks of pain. His left arm had taken the brunt of the impact and was grazed from shoulder to elbow, his T-shirt torn and dirty.

"Much as I enjoy your deference, it *would* be better for both of us if you stood up."

The delicious voice was beginning to sound impatient so Max hauled himself to his feet, clutching his wounded arm. He glanced up, then immediately cast his gaze down again. It was much easier to examine the paving than it was to meet those cold, stormy eyes. Blake Winters, CEO of Armacom, was an intimidating man at the best of times.

Max ran through what he knew about him in his head. He was only thirty and had built the organization from scratch. In nine years it had gone from a back-room operation to a multi-million pound global success story. Max, as well as every other Armacom employee, was fully aware of his back story and his reputation as an unrelenting hardass.

Max's usual shyness increased exponentially in the presence of his biggest crush. He'd heard Blake Winters speak at conferences and caught plenty of glimpses of him around the Armacom building but had never been this close to him before. He calculated they were roughly twelve inches apart, and that definitely constituted an invasion of personal space. Max took a step back. Blake closed the gap.

As far as making a good first impression went, Max had lost any chance of that. He was wet, smeared with dirt, bleeding and wearing a ragged pair of shorts and a torn T-shirt. He fumbled at the chinstrap of his helmet then yanked it off. Shaggy hair immediately fell into his eyes. He pushed it away with a shaking hand.

"Mr. Allenby, shouldn't you be in the lab by now?" Blake asked the question in a way that suggested he already knew the answer. Max doubted the man ever approached a conversation without knowing how it would end.

"How the hell do you know my name? Oh God, I said that out loud, didn't I?" Max glanced up cautiously and caught the edge of a smirk. He chewed on his lower lip debating what to say next that wouldn't increase the depth of the hole he was burying himself in. "Sorry. Puncture." He attempted to get a few coherent words out of his mouth. *Absolutely pathetic.* Max wanted to dissolve into the ground. Instead he found that he was unable to disengage his eye contact from Blake Winters. The man was absolutely gorgeous and everything that Max was not. Handsome, tall, self-assured, immaculately dressed… The list went on. Max felt his cock begin to swell and he nearly threw up at the thought that Winters might notice. He held his cycle helmet a bit lower and crossed his fingers.

"Blake, is everything okay?"

The chauffeur had joined them from the limo, and Max gaped at his use of Blake's first name.

"Who's this unfortunate specimen?"

Blake chuckled. "This, Sam, is one of our up-and-coming research scientists, believe it or not. He's the cyclist who rode into us."

"Ah. That explains it. They don't get let out of the lab very often, do they?" Sam picked up Max's bent bike and placed it in the rack.

"Well, this one certainly shouldn't be left alone, it seems he is a danger to himself and others."

Max swallowed. There were all kinds of nuances in Blake's tone that he didn't dare interpret too deeply.

"Hey, you hit me, not the other way round!" Attack was the best form of defense, right?

"You appeared out of nowhere, crossed two lanes at speed without signaling... You're lucky I trained in the military or I'd have squished you like a bug," Sam said. "I have good reflexes. The bumper just clipped your wheel. Your aerobatics were quite impressive, though." He chuckled.

"Um, thanks? I think." Max knew he'd been pedaling too fast and the only thing in his sights had been the bike rack. It was entirely his fault. "Hope I didn't dent the car."

"Little scrap like you? Barely left a mark—nothing that won't polish out with a bit of elbow grease."

Max couldn't decide whether to be insulted or relieved.

"Go ahead and park the car, Sam. I don't think I'll be needing you today so I'll see you tonight. Feel free to go back to the house after you've spoken to Amanda to get my schedule for next week."

"Sure, have a good day." Sam didn't ask any more questions. He gave Max a sympathetic grin, then headed back to the vehicle. As Sam drove away, Max gazed after him, sensing he'd lost an ally.

"Come with me, Max. Let's get that arm seen to. The grazes need to be cleaned up." Blake took a couple of strides

11

toward the building. When Max didn't follow he turned back. "Did you hit your head as well?"

"No, sir." The 'sir' slipped out easily and felt exactly right. "I can manage. I don't want to be any trouble—you must be busy?"

"It's Blake, and you need to learn to do as you're told. If I had somewhere else I needed to be, I would be there. Any questions?"

"No, sir."

"Good, then do as I say. Let's get inside. "

The reprimand sent an interesting tingle straight to Max's dick. Blake set off again, and this time Max followed. His shoulder throbbed horribly but the ache in his groin was worse. He shifted his bag onto his less damaged shoulder and hoped his limp would be put down to the accident.

The glass doors leading to the lobby slid open with a soft hiss. Blake strolled in like he owned the place, which made Max half snort, half giggle when he remembered that Blake did own it. The receptionist smiled and greeted Blake with a cheery, "Good morning, Mr. Winters." She ignored Max completely.

Max was used to that—the overly made-up girl probably didn't even know his name. It was the same with everyone they passed—he might as well have been invisible. Blake, however, knew everyone. He exchanged pleasantries and greetings but kept walking until they reached the first-aid room. Max gave an audible sigh of relief when Blake pushed open the door, revealing the room to be empty.

*The nurse is probably off having a coffee or visiting her first paper-cut casualty of the day.* Max's thought was a little uncharitable but he was sore and being so close to Blake was making him nervous and edgy.

"I can just wait here for the nurse to come back, sir. You don't have to..."

"Sit."

Max's attempt to deflect Blake was cut off by the perfunctory command. He sat. Blake's tone suggested that

12

any other response would not be sensible or conducive to Max's career prospects. He'd lay money that if the man had a dog he'd be the best-trained mutt in the state. He watched in bewilderment as Blake rummaged in a cupboard. He produced a bright green first-aid box and seconds later was sitting opposite him pouring liquid antiseptic onto a sterile gauze pad.

"This will probably hurt." He began to dab at the grazes on Max's arm.

"Fuck, that stings!" Max yelped. "Sorry, I didn't mean to be an ungrateful patient." He gritted his teeth and tried to keep still.

Undeterred, Blake ignored Max's squirming and kept going until the wounds were clean of dirt and grit.

"You picked up half the asphalt. It would definitely have gotten infected if the wounds closed over all that muck. Better some pain now than a course of antibiotics later."

"Yes, sir. Thank you."

Blake applied a dressing and taped it in place. Max decided that it was his imagination when Blake's touch lingered a bit too long. He wondered if there was any kind of pill that could deflate a raging erection—and if there was, where he could get one in the next thirty seconds. *There's stuff for getting it up, there has to be something for getting the damn thing down as well.*

"There. All better. I assume you have a change of clothes with you?" Blake asked, his expression dubious.

Max slipped off his stool and edged toward the door. "Yes, I do. In my bag. Thanks for your help, sir. I really appreciate it." He yanked open the door and ran before Blake could stop him or say another word—or spot his very inconvenient erection. His luck held and he made it to the men's locker room without encountering any curious colleagues. He stripped off his filthy clothes, nudging them into a pile with his toe. He doubted they were salvageable, but they would have to do for the journey home that evening. He padded into the showers, took the first cubicle

13

then stood beneath the spray, arm sticking out awkwardly to keep his dressing dry.

"Fuck, fuck, fuck, bloody fuck!" Max's wry smile came with the realization that he had sworn more in that single morning than he had all year. He didn't usually resort to expletives but he gave himself a pass for the day—the circumstances were exceptional. He slicked his hand with gel from the pump dispenser on the wall, then grabbed his aching cock. He had to give himself some relief—every thought of Blake Winters administering first aid, his firm but gentle touch, made him harder and there was no way he could go into the lab with a stiffy that even his lab coat wouldn't be able to disguise. He was already going to be in so much trouble that a few extra minutes were not going to make things any worse.

He slid his hand up and down, feeling the tremors run down his spine, making his legs shake. It wasn't going to take long. He squeezed a little harder, punishing himself for his lack of self-control. He wondered what it would be like to have Blake's hand gripping him rather than his own. That thought was enough. Max came with a low moan and an artistic splatter across the tiles. That dealt with his physical problem but was no help at all when it came to deleting Blake's image from the inside of his eyelids, where it seemed to be indelibly printed. The shower washed away the evidence of his release, and once his legs had stopped shaking he finished washing.

The changing rooms remained mercifully empty as Max toweled himself dry and dressed in his crumpled work clothes. Ironing was not one of his favorite chores and he was thankful that his lab coat covered a multitude of sins. He felt strangely nervous, half expecting Blake Winters to appear around a corner at any moment. He had no idea what he would do if that were to happen. Turn into a stammering, blushing wreck again probably. Blake would surely have his own executive bathroom anyway—all shiny marble and gold taps. He wouldn't need to set foot

14

anywhere near the communal showers.

Max shoved his tattered, muddy cycling kit into a locker. He grabbed his lab coat from its hook then, armed with a semblance of professionalism, he headed off to face his boss. Dr. Ella Preston was a bitch of the first order. If it weren't for the fact that Max loved his work and the excellent research facilities that Armacom offered, he probably would have caved in and left the company by now. He'd had other offers but wanted to stay at least until he'd finished his doctorate, which Armacom was funding.

Dr. Preston found fault with everything he did, constantly sniping away at how inadequate he was. Even worse, Max knew damn well that she had been passing his work off as her own. He just couldn't prove it, and as she was so fond of saying, they were all supposed to be part of one collaborative team. Theoretically they all worked for the benefit of Armacom, not their own selfish gratification. Max suspected that Dr. Preston interpreted that as her taking the credit for everything the team toiled hard to produce.

He tapped his code into the lab's security pad and pushed the door open, nerves tingling. He made it to his workstation, fired up his computer and got to work. There was no sign of his nemesis. He was just beginning to relax and think he'd gotten away with his tardiness for once when a sharp tap on his shoulder nearly shocked him into falling off his seat. The legs of his stool rocked back and forth, before finally settling where they should be. He really didn't need any more injuries—his body ached enough as it was. He planted his feet on the floor for better stability.

"Nice of you to join us, Mr. Allenby." Sarcasm dripped from Ella Preston's every word.

He swiveled around to face her. "I'm sorry I was late, I had to stop and fix a puncture. There was a nail…"

"And then you had an accident, I understand?"

Max nodded, wondering how she knew. "A car hit me outside, at the front of the building."

"I had a call from Mr. Winter's PA informing me that you

would be delayed and that it would be wise to keep an eye on you in case you had sustained a head injury."

"Oh." Max couldn't think of anything else to say. Blake had probably saved him from a morning of verbal abuse. That gave him superhero status.

"Hmm. *Did* you hit your head? I doubt anyone would notice the difference." Dr Preston's smile was as fake as her tan. "Do you have a headache?"

*That's right, lace concern with poison.* Max fidgeted unhappily. "I hurt my arm. I don't remember hitting my head, but then I don't suppose I would. I was wearing my helmet."

She grunted and turned away. "You can make up the time this evening. Just because the boss seems to be concerned about you doesn't mean you can slack off."

Max breathed a sigh of relief and got back to work. Thanks to Blake he'd gotten off lightly. It had been kind of him to call, or rather to ask his PA to do it. Max wondered what Blake was doing at that moment then shook his head. He didn't have time to be daydreaming about Blake Winters.

He had reams of data to analyze, something he usually enjoyed. He likened it to unraveling a puzzle, teasing out threads of information hidden within spreadsheets of anonymous numbers. But this morning he couldn't focus on anything. Figures blurred in front of his eyes and he began to wonder if there *was* a dent in his skull.

His thoughts kept drifting to Blake, his steely eyes, stern expression and gruff voice. Max knew the man would feature in his dreams that night. He was already aware that Blake was gay, it wasn't a secret, but he had no idea if he was single. Probably not—he was rich and gorgeous—he probably had his pick of willing lovers. But then perhaps he wasn't interested in 'willing'. Blake Winters oozed dominance from every pore, and Max suspected he might prefer a more challenging conquest. His lips twitched into a wry smile. Submitting to a man like Blake would be a dream come true but he would never, ever have the courage

16

to approach him voluntarily, and it was unlikely that their paths would cross again.

Max was still smiling, gazing off into nowhere, when the lab door banged open and Armacom's head of security marched up to him.

"You had an accident. Why the fuck didn't you ring me?"

Max poked his tongue out. "Because you're my brother, not my mom, Justin, that's why. Not that I would have rung Mom either. It's not like I broke any bones or anything."

In Max's opinion, their mother must have planted Justin in fertilizer when he was a child. Max could have done with a few of his extra inches of height. Now he was using it to loom.

"I had to find out you were hurt from my boss, for pity's sake!" Justin growled.

Max's face heated as his colleagues sent amused, vaguely sympathetic glances his way. "But Blake Winters is your boss..."

"Yes, he is, genius. He told me that he had to scrape you off the pavement this morning after you attempted to mangle his BMW!"

Max lost the ability to speak.

"Show me," Justin demanded.

"No! I'm not going to show you, Justin." Indignation restored Max's voice. "I did not mangle his car, he hit me! At least his chauffeur did. Besides, it's just a scrape. And some bruises. I'm twenty-four, not seven! I can look after myself."

"You could have fooled me." Justin folded his arms across his broad chest, and Max grinned — the two of them couldn't have been more different. Justin was six feet four, with a shaved head, and had muscles on his muscles. Max was five feet ten, slight, with long hair and a face too pretty to be masculine. Justin was married and had four kids. Max had known he preferred boys since he was fourteen. Sometimes he wondered if one of them was adopted but their dad insisted he had witnessed both births himself.

17

Physically, Justin took after their father while Max was more like their mother. He had her blonde hair and light blue eyes. Justin was confident and outgoing, Max was shy and reserved, but both brothers had inherited their dad's dry sense of humor.

"If I want someone to fuss over me, I'll ring Mom. Now go away and leave me alone, Justin, I already have to work late to make up for this morning—you'll get me into even more trouble!"

Justin smirked. "Dr. Preston has a thing for me. I think she gets frustrated being surrounded by all you geeks."

"I need brain bleach. You've just planted images in my head that could damage me for life. I hope you're proud of yourself, big brother."

Justin reached out and ruffled Max's hair. "Just look after yourself, okay? Be careful cycling home tonight."

"Yeah, yeah... And I'll carry a hanky and wear clean underwear just in case."

Justin smacked his head. "Cheeky brat. Call me when you get in this evening."

Max rubbed the sore spot, making his hair even messier. "Fine. Now clear off and leave me in peace."

Justin winked at Dr. Preston, making her blush the shade of a ripe tomato. Max bent over his work, hiding a snigger. Justin was incorrigible and had got Max into trouble so many times during their childhood that Max had lost count. Justin was very protective of his little brother, though, just as he was of Armacom and its employees. He was perfect for his job. Max still stuck his tongue out at Justin's retreating back.

He felt a little stir of envy that Justin got to see Blake Winters every day while he was stuck in the clinical atmosphere of the lab with Ella Preston as his boss. He sighed. Why be jealous? Blake could be perched on the stool next to him and he wouldn't have a clue what to say to him. In chemical terms, Max would have all the reactivity of an inert gas while Blake would definitely explode alongside the potent heavy metals.

The day dragged by as if Old Father Time were on a permanent coffee break. For once, Dr. Preston left Max alone, though he did catch her glaring at him from a distance several times. He had only grabbed a fifteen-minute lunch break, scarfing down a banana and a packet of crisps, so by the time he came to pack up at the end of the day his stomach was grumbling loudly.

There was nobody else left in the lab so Max checked everything that needed to be was switched off and turned out the lights. He wandered back to the locker room and changed into his cycling kit with a grimace. His shorts were dirty and torn and his T-shirt was smeared with blood, but better that than ruin his decent work trousers on the ride home. He swapped his shoes for muddy sneakers, stowed his work clothes in his backpack then headed out to the bike racks.

"Great, just great." He scowled at the abysmal weather. It was dark and it was raining so hard that he thought New Hampshire might be trying to compete with Mumbai in monsoon season. He pulled his bike from its metal stand and grimaced as pain shot through his shoulder. He bit his lip to stop himself from crying out like a baby. He very nearly did start sobbing, though, when, after twenty minutes of poking and prodding, he had to accept how unrideable his bike was. One wheel was buckled and needed replacing. There was no way he was going to be able to get home on it. He shoved it back into the rack in disgust, sat on the wet ground and rested his head in his hands. Water soaked through his shorts and underwear but he didn't care. His day couldn't get any worse. He would have to ring Justin and beg a lift – the plan of last, desperate resort.

Shaking with cold, he pulled his mobile out of the back pocket of his little pack only to find that the battery had died. He stared up at the sky, letting the raindrops splash across his face, and shook his head. "I'm not sure what I've done to deserve this, but could you please give me a fucking break?"

Footsteps came to a halt behind him. "I'm not sure that cursing at the Almighty is going to get you very far."

"Oh fuck…" Max swiveled around on his ass.

Blake Winters smirked down at him. He was wearing a raincoat and holding a black umbrella. "Most of my staff tend to avoid swearing at me too, Max, for good reason."

Max scrambled awkwardly to his feet. His shorts were sticking to his ass and his T-shirt had adhered to his chest. Water slid down his nose and plopped to the ground. "Sorry." He felt like a naughty schoolboy in front of the headmaster. His stomach rumbled, adding to his misery.

"Sam's just bringing the car round. I'll take you home." Blake held out his umbrella so that it gave Max some shelter from the downpour.

"That's not necessary, sir, really. I can just call my brother and he'll…"

"That wasn't a suggestion, Max. I'm sure the last thing you want to do is drag Justin away from his family." Blake spoke in such a way that Max's cock jerked. Impressive considering how wet and cold he was. The man was just so…in control.

The car swept smoothly to the curb in front of them.

"I don't expect Sam to open doors for me, so get in." Blake walked around the car and climbed in the other side.

Max twisted the bottom of his T-shirt, wringing some of the moisture from it. He sighed and opened the door closest to him. The interior was warm and inviting, so why did he feel like he was climbing into a trap? He got in anyway — Blake Winters' web was preferable to dying of hypothermia.

"The advantage of leather seats is that they wipe clean," Blake said.

Max tried to make himself as small as possible, feeling like a microbe under a microscope.

"Though it might be an idea to shut the door."

Max pulled the car door closed and tried to remember how to breathe. With any luck he'd lose consciousness and

20

wake up on his own doorstep. *There's no place like home. There's no place like home. Tap my heels together. God, I'm losing it. Where the fuck are those ruby slippers when I need them?*

# Chapter Two

Blake Winters sat in the back of his car and tried to hold on to his composure, something he was rarely inclined to let slip. Max Allenby was one of the prettiest young men he'd come across, and the first to make a lasting impression on him. Blake had maintained an interest in his progress since he'd joined Armacom. Max Allenby had great potential. He also had a perfect air of vulnerability offset by resigned acceptance that the world was apt to rain on his parade.

*An apt analogy in today's downpour.* Blake wondered if Max had any idea what a temptation he presented with wet fabric clinging to his lean body. The cold had hardened his nipples into peaks that showed dark through a T-shirt made virtually transparent by the rain. Blake had to force himself not to lick his lips—how he would love to clamp those sweet little nubs and make the boy squirm. Max smelled of fresh summer rain and a hint of herbs. The stimulation to Blake's senses was a heady combination.

He stole a sidelong glance at his shivering companion. Max was at least half hard. Those ridiculous shorts hid nothing, as Blake had already witnessed that morning. Max had tried to conceal his arousal then too, but Blake had noticed. How could he not? He assumed the physical reaction meant that Max was attracted to him, even if his emotions were tempered somewhat by shyness and a touch of fear. Blake wanted to comfort him, to reassure him that all would be fine. Everything about Max shrieked submissive but Blake had no idea whether or not Max recognized that trait in himself let alone accepted it. He suspected that it might have to be coaxed from him. Inside, Blake smiled—

he had never been one to resist a challenge. He needed the fresh inspiration a fledgling submissive would bring. Max would be the perfect subject.

Blake unclipped his seatbelt, leaned forward then shrugged off his top coat and jacket. His coat was damp so he put it to one side, but his jacket was warm and dry. "Here, put this on before you destroy the car's suspension with all that shaking." He put the garment on the seat between him and Max, not wanting to assume that his touch would be welcome.

Max blinked, then shook his head. "I can't, I'll ruin it. I'm a bit damp." His teeth were chattering and there was a faint blue tinge to his skin even in the warmth of the car.

Blake sighed but reined in his impatience. He released Max's seatbelt then slid across the seat and put his jacket around Max's shoulders. "I've seen pond life drier than you are. You're too stubborn for your own good." He pressed the backs of his fingers against Max's forearm—his skin was clammy and very cold. "We need to get you properly warm, you're bordering on hypothermic." He caught Sam's eye in the rear-view mirror. "Change of plan. Let's go to Watersmeet first please, Sam. It's farther than Max's place, but I don't think he should be left alone just yet."

Sam gave him a brief thumbs up. Blake laid his topcoat over Max's bare legs then refastened his seatbelt. The metal catch closed with a satisfying clunk. "There. Safely strapped in."

"I don't want to put you to any trouble, sir," Max said.

"Nonsense. I have to make sure you're okay and my house is only just outside of town. I can easily drive you home later. I won't take no for an answer, Max."

Even in the dimly lit interior of the car, Blake could make out what a beautiful blue Max's eyes were—the soft shade of cornflowers. They widened and he nibbled at a lower lip that looked like it got a lot of similar abuse. He pulled at the seatbelt with his slim fingers, as if to check that it could still be released. The broad black straps looked delicious across

23

Max's body. Blake replaced them in his mind with silken ropes and his cock began to swell. He idly wondered how Max might respond to bindings that could not be so easily removed. Would he struggle or would the restriction calm him?

Blake sat back and relaxed, his head filled with possibilities. Of course Max might be totally unaware of the joys of a D/s lifestyle. He might prefer holding hands in the park or cuddling on the sofa in front of a roaring fire. Both could be accommodated. Even a short stroll became a whole new experience when there was a vibrating plug up your ass, and snuggling was always a nice way to take the sting out of a spanking. Blake realized that he was tapping his knee and forced himself to become still. He needed to be calm and focused, not drowning in dreams that had yet to be realized.

The car slowed and gravel crunched beneath the wheels as they turned into the drive leading to Watersmeet. Blake's home was his pride and joy. He had designed it himself — driving the architect mad as he attempted to translate his ideas into something the poor man could work with. The end result was worth every second spent poring over drawings and diagrams, and all the times Blake had trudged around a building site in wellies wondering why things weren't progressing faster. He was looking forward to showing Max around. *First things first, get your priorities right, Blake.* Max needed warmth and, judging by the sounds issuing from the direction of his stomach, food. The man needed a keeper — it was clear he didn't have any idea how to take care of himself properly.

Security lights blinked on as Sam parked in front of the triple garage block and turned off the ignition.

"Thanks, Sam, that will be all for tonight," Blake dismissed the chauffeur. "If Max wants to go home later I'll drive him myself."

Max swiveled in his seat. "Okay, boss. Usual time in the morning?"

"Yes, that will be fine. Friday tomorrow. Only one more day and then you'll be off to sun, sea and relaxation."

Sam grinned. "Between the missus and the kids, I'm not sure it's going to be that relaxing. I'll probably need another break to get over it. Change of scenery and some sun will be good, though."

"Well, I'll be glad to get you back." Blake was quite capable of driving himself around but preferred to work while he traveled. During office hours, he was rarely alone and the journeys to and from Armacom provided an opportunity to make calls, plan and think. Running his own business could become all-consuming and he was as strict as he could be about maintaining some distance once he got home. Sam might seem like a rich man's indulgence, but he helped keep Blake sane.

Blake climbed out of the car and shivered—the temperature had dropped significantly but at least it was no longer raining. Max looked bedraggled and a bit unsteady on his feet as he got out. All Blake's protective instincts kicked in. He circled Max's slim waist with one arm and took some of his weight. Max didn't complain or resist, so Blake took that as acceptance. He tightened his grip and walked Max to the house.

Once inside, he took his shaking charge straight to one of the guest bedrooms on the first floor—the one with the biggest en-suite bathroom and a luxurious freestanding tub. Blake maneuvered Max into the room and settled him in a basket chair in the corner. Tremors wracked Max's slender frame. He hugged himself but it had no effect on his chattering teeth.

Rolling up his shirtsleeves, Blake set about preparing a hot bath. He turned the faucet on full and dumped a generous splash of bath oil beneath the torrent. Soon the room was filled with steam and the delicate scent of citrus. He swirled the water around, checking the temperature. Satisfied, he straightened.

"Stand up, Max, I have to get you out of your wet clothes."

25

Max stood obediently, but when Blake started to undress him, he wrapped his arms around himself defensively. Blake gave him the same look he gave to business rivals who attempted hostile takeovers of his company. Max's eyes widened and he dropped his arms to his sides and remained still while Blake removed his borrowed jacket, filthy T-shirt and ripped shorts. He pulled free the sodden laces on Max's sneakers then tapped a bare ankle, prompting Max to remove them. Stripping Max's tight, black underwear might be a step too far, though he really, *really* wanted to. Max's expression was one of defeat. Blake knew instinctively that there would be no resistance, but it wasn't the time. Max was far too vulnerable, and Blake had no intention of taking advantage. He needed to build trust between them, not destroy it.

"Take your time. Your nerve endings are going to believe the water is scalding hot because you're so cold, but you need to get in and soak until your body temperature rises. There's a robe on the back of the door you can borrow. I'm going to make us something to eat, so come and find me in the kitchen when you're done. Down the stairs, turn left, follow the hall." Was it his imagination or did Max look disappointed that he hadn't stripped him naked? It could be wishful thinking but his instincts were usually correct. Max scuffed his bare toes into the bath mat.

Blake picked up Max's discarded clothes. "These are heading for the incinerator. You have your work clothes with you?"

"Yes, in my bag." Max pointed at a soggy looking backpack.

"They must be damp, if not soaked through. I'll throw them in the drier."

"Thanks. You're being very kind, sir." He bent and dipped his hand in the water, testing it.

Blake gave him the benefit of the doubt and decided the move wasn't deliberate. If it had been, then presenting his ass in such a blatant fashion would have earned Max a spanking. He left him to get on with his bath, pulling the door closed behind him. Blake allowed himself a satisfied smile. Leaving Max alone had been the appropriate decision, but Max was sending all the right signals that he was open to more.

Humming quietly, Blake headed to the kitchen. It was one of his favorite rooms—a place he could relax. Everything was immaculately clean and smelled faintly of lemons. It wasn't of his doing. Blake employed a married couple to maintain Watersmeet, and they did a consistently excellent job. Ada Smith did the cleaning, organized the laundry service and did his grocery shopping while her husband Ron took care of maintenance and supervised the gardeners. In total, Blake employed five domestic staff and they were worth every penny. Ada always stocked the freezer with home-made meals that he could reheat, but he liked to cook when he had time. He raided the fridge, looking for inspiration for a quick meal—nothing too fancy. He spotted some fresh asparagus tips and French beans. It crossed his mind that Max might be vegetarian so he erred on the side of caution and decided on spring vegetable pasta in a light cheese sauce.

Pottering around, preparing ingredients and setting water to boil, Blake almost managed to forget that Max was, at that moment, floating in his bathtub. Naked, pale skin slick with scented oil, blond hair floating on the water. He *almost* managed to forget, but not quite. He could picture Max's flaccid cock lifted by ripples in the water, and lean muscles gradually relaxing as the chill was soaked away.

Losing track of what he was doing completely, he dropped a spoon on the tiled floor. "Damn it!" He gave a short, self-deprecating laugh. He had been denying himself the pleasures of a tender young submissive for far too long. If he was going to earn Max's trust, he had to stay in control of his emotions.

Blake had very few vices. He didn't smoke, had never done drugs, occasionally indulged in the odd glass of good wine but hadn't been drunk since his student days. He recognized his faults—he was jealously possessive of his lovers, a control freak of the highest order at home and at work, and especially in the bedroom. He liked to give orders and was absolutely merciless in the boardroom. In short, those who didn't know him well probably considered him an utter bastard. He was also highly intelligent and a shrewd, instinctive businessman—qualities that had made him extremely rich. He could sell Armacom and retire for life if he wanted to but knew that the ethical practices he employed would never be continued by anyone else because they reduced profit margins. He developed technology only for defensive use—researching the latest experimental compounds that could be used in armor and clothing to protect soldiers, policemen and firefighters around the world.

But at that moment, all that mattered was creating the perfect al dente texture for his pasta and faultlessly seasoning the sauce so that Max would enjoy it. The food was almost ready. Blake laid two place settings at the dining room table. Chilled wine and water were waiting in the fridge. There was only one thing missing. One person.

"Where the heck is he?" Blake muttered. For a brief moment he panicked—had Max fallen asleep in the bath? "I shouldn't have left him alone." He quelled his nerves with a couple of sips of water then went to find his guest.

Wrapped in a chocolate brown robe, feet bare, Max was padding down the corridor toward the kitchen. Blake repressed a sigh of relief and settled for a look of mild reproof. "I was wondering where you were. How are you feeling?"

Max pulled the thick, brown fabric more closely around himself, playing with the end of the belt. "Sorry, sir. It was just so warm and relaxing, I didn't want to get out of the water. I only have a shower at home so it was a real luxury. I feel much better, thank you."

That had to be the most words Max had ever managed to

string together in Blake's presence. Apparently shocked by his own boldness, he subsided into silence.

"I'm glad you enjoyed it. I like a good soak myself every now and again." Max's gratitude sent a pleasant tingle down his spine. "I hope you're hungry because dinner is ready." He turned away to hide his smug, self-satisfied grin. Max was safe and more relaxed than Blake had ever seen him. He also looked absolutely adorable wrapped in that robe. One tug on the belt and Blake would get the view he craved, and Christ was he tempted. He should get some kind of award for restraint—he definitely deserved it as he left Max in the dining room and went to fetch their meal. He took a carafe of iced water in first. "You may pour— unless you would prefer something stronger?"

Max sat on the edge of his chair, his feet tucked up on the crossbar. He shook his head, damp hair glistening. "I don't drink. I discovered a few years ago that half a pint of beer is all it takes to make me act like an idiot so I haven't bothered since. It makes me a really cheap date." He ducked his head. "Oh God… I didn't mean… That is, that's what Justin always says."

"Your big brother does have a way with words, but fortunately I don't need to economize when it comes to dating, Max." Blake chuckled.

"I wasn't suggesting…" Max's voice trembled, and Blake wondered if he was about to cry.

"I know you weren't." He gave him some space and went to fetch the pasta. By the time Blake returned, Max had composed himself and managed to pour two glasses of water without spilling or breaking anything. He eyed the food hungrily.

"That looks great. I'm ravenous." He ran the tip of his tongue over his lower lip.

"Didn't you eat today?" Blake asked, trying not to make the question sound like a criticism.

"I missed breakfast, and I only had time for a snack at lunchtime because I didn't want to have to work even later.

I was making up time for being late in," Max replied.

"Then it's no wonder your stomach is more vocal than the rest of you. You're to eat properly in future." Blake waited to see how Max would react to the order.

"Yes, sir." There wasn't a trace of sarcasm in Max's response.

"Tuck in, there's no need to stand on ceremony." Blake followed his own advice and spooned some pasta onto his plate. He pushed the serving dish toward Max. "Help yourself." He tried not to stare at Max too much, but the boy moved so prettily that it was hard not to.

Each movement was precise and graceful. He ate with obvious enjoyment, and for a while, with food to distract him, his anxiety seemed to diminish. Blake didn't tax him with conversation or questions—he let him eat in peace. Max finally pushed his plate away. There was no more reason for silence. Blake gave Max an appraising look. "It's late. You're welcome to stay here tonight. The guest rooms are always made up."

"That's very kind, sir, but I can't. I need to go home," Max said, his gaze darting around the room—anywhere but at Blake.

"Can't or won't? And I've already told you that it's not necessary to call me sir. That is, unless you...choose to." Max was resting one of his hands on the table. Blake placed his hand over Max's, just for a moment.

Max gasped and jerked away like he'd been stung, but a beautiful blush stained his cheek. "I really mustn't stay... Sir." The last word was whispered very quietly.

That tiny, three-letter word was all Blake needed to hear. Regardless of anything Max said from then on, he was snared, and they both knew it. Getting him to act on his feelings was a whole different issue, but Blake knew that he just had to use the right motivation and Max would be his. He would let Max think that he had escaped, give him time to become less guarded, then cut off all his exits. It was a strategy that worked in the boardroom, and Blake had no reason to doubt that it would work on Max too.

# Chapter Three

Armacom's staff cafeteria was light, airy and totally different from the sterile atmosphere of the research labs. The white tables were circular and the comfy swivel chairs that surrounded them a whole rainbow of bright colors. Max sat in a lilac one. Across the table, Justin's seat was bright red. It was a cheery space but Max wasn't feeling all that positive. He stared intently at the contents of his mug in an attempt to identify them.

"It's peppermint tea, Max, it's not scary." Justin quirked an eyebrow.

"It looks like pond water. Smells good, though. Perhaps if I close my eyes?" Max really didn't trust the appearance of the greenish liquid swirling in his mug. He was a scientist — he preferred to know the chemical composition of things he consumed.

"Just drink it, you wimp. It'll make a change from that leaded fuel you pass off as coffee." Justin took a long swallow of his own identical drink.

"Fine. Don't say I never try anything new." Max took a tentative sip and his frown gradually morphed into a smile.

"See. Told you so," Justin crowed.

"You sound like a three year old, Justin, there's no need to be smug. It is surprisingly nice, though it looks disgusting." Max took another sip, both hands wrapped around the mug. "Now, are you going to tell me why you've dragged me away from impact testing my latest body armor?" As he waited for an explanation, Max couldn't decide whether Justin's expression was anxious or just a bit sheepish. His brother was uncharacteristically hesitant and that usually meant bad news.

"What's wrong? Are the kids okay? And Helen?" Now Max was getting concerned. "You're scaring me!"

"They're all fine, so stop worrying. It's just… Well, I've got myself into a bit of a bind and I need you to help get me out of it." Justin was doing his best impression of a hurt puppy, blinking big sad eyes at Max.

It was so out of character that Max couldn't help but laugh. "It must be bad! Now what do you need me to do to get your sorry ass out of trouble this time?"

"I may have mentioned to Blake that you liked him. That's all." Justin wouldn't make eye contact.

"You did what?" Max shouted, and was half out of his chair, intent on damaging his only sibling. He'd been too loud and everyone in range was watching with interest. Max thought it might even be worth the gossip if he and Justin ended up scrapping on the floor.

"The fact that has got you so riled tells me I didn't lie." Justin smirked. "You've been mooning over him for ages. We were talking and he told me about taking you back to his place to dry out. Somehow we got on to types that appealed to us. I confessed to liking redheads. He prefers blonds."

Max pictured his sister-in-law's bright copper curls. "I'm sure your preference wasn't that much of a surprise."

"I let slip that you had a thing for…well, for him."

Max took a few calming breaths. "I can't believe you did that. What did he say?"

"I'm not going to tell you, I don't betray confidences, but I thought you ought to know."

Max's jaw dropped. "You hypocritical oaf. I don't recall saying you could gossip about my personal fantasies."

"You'll thank me one day."

"Tell me, Justin. I'm a chemist, remember—I'll cook up something that'll shrivel your balls if you don't."

"I really can't tell you, but Blake will probably speak to you himself. Just keep an open mind when he does. Blake

33

can be…intense." Justin was already pushing his chair back.

"But what's he going to say and when? I'm a scientist. I need facts, not unbelievably irritating maybes from a brother with a much-reduced lifespan." Max was starting to get properly annoyed. "You'd better not be yanking my chain."

"Would I do that to you?"

Justin stood, then strolled away without looking back. Max realized that he must resemble some weird species of fish as his mouth gaped open again. The question did not deserve the courtesy of an answer. He clamped his lips shut and shrugged. Justin would never tell him anything else if he didn't want to. He was as immovable as granite when it came to confidentiality. Max would just have to wait and see. He went back to his lab, curiosity, tinged with a flavor of worry, distracting him.

The day proved to be deadly dull, and Max came to the conclusion that Justin had been messing around. Blake did not appear at the lab door. The most exciting thing that happened was a colleague asking if she could borrow his highlighter. Max immersed himself in work and forgot all about Justin's mysterious drama. The clock ticked round to four. He was writing up the day's test results and double-checking his data when he overheard the end of a conversation his boss was having on the telephone.

"Yes, I suppose I can spare him if it's that important. Fine, no problem. I'll let him know." Dr. Preston couldn't sound any more grudging if she tried.

Max was the only 'him' in the lab at that time so it wasn't a great surprise when Dr. Preston beckoned him over in her usual imperious fashion. She'd make a great egomaniac dictator for some unfortunate country if she ever fancied a career change.

"You're wanted in the chief executive's office, so tidy yourself up and get over there."

"Umm, why?" Max, stomach churning, frantically tried to think of anything he'd done wrong.

34

"How should I know? The big man issues a summons — you do as you're told. Stop asking stupid questions and move."

Dr. Preston was clearly annoyed. She probably thought she should be the one heading over there rather than Max.

"Try not to act like an idiot, you represent this lab, God help us."

Max felt suddenly nervous. Blake Winters had driven him home less than twenty-four hours ago and he had neither heard from the man nor seen him since. After their dinner, Max had changed into his crumpled but dry work clothes and given Blake back his robe. The car ride hadn't taken long, but Max had been painfully hard the whole time. Sitting so close to Blake was torment, especially as Blake had brushed Max's knee every time he'd changed gear. Max suspected it had been deliberate — he didn't think Blake ever did anything unintentionally.

They'd parted with a brief goodbye — Blake hadn't even got out of the car. In the morning, Max had wondered if he had dreamed the whole experience. Now his stomach was in knots at the thought of seeing Blake again — had he misinterpreted the hints and glances? If Blake was as dominant as Max suspected, would he even be interested in someone as shy and reserved as Max? He'd probably prefer a bratty, confident sub who knew exactly what he wanted and had at least some vague idea of what the hell he was doing.

Max took off his lab coat and hung it on a peg. His plain black trousers were clean and he'd managed not to drop anything down his shirt, though it was a bit rumpled. He finger-combed his hair — there was no redeeming the tangled mess without professional assistance. At least he'd found time to shave that morning, stubble just made him look even scruffier. He hesitated, hoping against hope that Dr. Preston would find a reason for him to stay, but she ignored him completely. He grabbed a notepad and pen then left the office with a resigned sigh.

35

Blake's office was on the other side of the building, tucked into a corner near the conference suite. His personal assistant, Amanda Cross, had her own space in an outer room and was well known for her tendency to act like a rabid Rottweiler with socialization issues. Getting to see Blake without an appointment or invitation was as difficult as getting in to see the President. Max approached her desk with some trepidation. If this was all a mistake then he was about to get dismissed with a flea in his ear. He braced himself but Amanda greeted him with a warm smile.

"He's expecting you, Mr. Allenby, please go straight in. Can I bring you any refreshments?"

"No thank you," Max refused. His throat was very dry but he knew that any cup or glass he held would shake so badly that the contents would end up all over him. He knocked lightly on Blake's door and pushed it open.

"It's just a door, Max, all you have to do is walk through it."

Blake's sarcasm pushed Max into action. He edged into the office, closed the door behind him and took a curious look around Blake's territory. The room was plain and functional, decorated in exactly the same way as all the other offices in the building. There was a small meeting table in a corner encircled by four chairs. A low bookcase stood beneath one of the windows, a vase of fresh flowers centered on the top of it. Blake's desk was a sheet of smoky glass on tubular steel legs, and other than a laptop, notepad and pen it was completely clear. Max thought about the clutter on his own small table in the lab and resolved to tidy up a bit.

Blake's only apparent concession to status was the large leather chair he was sitting in. Max felt a small pang of envy—his own stool was practical for the lab environment but not very kind to his ass. He had looked everywhere but at Blake and had run out of reasons to examine anything else. There was no chair in front of the desk so he stood, clasped his shaking hands behind his back and nervously

36

raised his eyes. His face began to heat and so did his cock — there was nothing he could do to stop it. Blake was wearing a fitted white shirt that showed off his broad shoulders and firm chest to perfection. But that wasn't the problem. He was also wearing dark-rimmed glasses that gave him a sexy intellectual look. Max had always had a thing for men in specs, something to do with his inner geek probably. He really wished he could sit down — his legs were turning to jelly. Blake looked so stern and gorgeous and... Hell, Max couldn't think straight. He dug his fingernails into the palm of his hand — perhaps pain would provide a suitable distraction because imagining Dr. Preston in the nude wasn't helping in the least.

Blake stood and walked around his desk. He pulled a chair over from the small meeting area and placed it behind Max's legs.

"Sit before you fall down, Max." The amusement in his voice was clear, but Max didn't care.

He sat with some relief but his nerves resurfaced when Blake didn't return to his chair but leaned back against his desk. The position pushed his crotch forward, and though his charcoal gray trousers were not tight, his erection was clearly evident.

Max swallowed and reflected that maybe a glass of water wouldn't have been a bad idea — either for drinking to soothe his dry throat or for throwing over his own head to cool his burning face. Blake was so close... He had to fight his urge to lean forward and nuzzle against his enticing bulge.

"Testing today went well?" Blake asked.

"No, I mean yes, I mean... The results weren't what I expected, sir. I need to do more tests." The neural receptors that controlled Max's ability to speak were definitely damaged. He stumbled over his words, confused that work was still a part of his life.

"Well, I look forward to your report. I firmly believe in testing to the limit, don't you?" Blake's smile could only be

37

described as wolfish.

Max shivered. He had a feeling that the conversation had moved on but Blake hadn't bothered to give him the agenda.

"Yes, sir, we need to know the limitations of the product."

"We do indeed." Blake leaned forward and brushed a stray strand of hair from Max's cheek.

Max could smell him, all spicy and warm, his touch so gentle. He had to get away or he was going to come there and then.

"Was there something else you wanted, sir?" There had to be—to Max's knowledge, Blake had never personally enquired about testing results before.

"Yes, Max, there is." Blake moved back behind his desk and sat in his chair, completely relaxed. "Your brother and I have been talking."

Max groaned. "Whatever he said, sir, I hope you ignored him. Justin has an overactive imagination."

"Well, he mentioned that you liked me so I hope he wasn't making it up." Blake raised an eyebrow.

"No, sir. I mean yes, sir. I mean… It's none of his business, sir. He shouldn't have said anything."

"I don't suppose he should. However, information always has value, don't you think?"

"In certain circumstances, sir, yes it does."

"Now I know how you feel, I need to do something about it."

Max swallowed hard. Was he about to get fired? "Oh?"

"I'd like to involve you in a small experiment, Max."

Max blinked. He was having trouble keeping up. If Blake needed something scientific then he could deal with that. "What kind of parameters, sir?"

"It's vital work. It could affect both our futures depending on the outcome."

Max's intellectual curiosity perked up. "I'd be glad to help if I can, sir."

"That's good, because this experiment, or perhaps trial

38

would be a better description, definitely requires both of us."

"Okay," Max said, drawing out the word.

"How would you feel about testing the possibilities of a relationship between us? Under strictly controlled conditions of course." Blake seemed to put an inordinate amount of emphasis on the word 'strictly'.

"I don't understand, sir."

"Perhaps I didn't make myself clear," Blake said. "I would like to date you, Max."

Max jabbed his biro into his notepad. "You would?"

"Yes, I believe we are well suited."

"I don't think you're talking about dinner and a movie, though, are you, sir?" Max asked.

Blake smiled. "No, though I'm sure that would be pleasant. Do you know what a Dominant is, Max?"

"I… Is it hot in here?" Max wished once more that he'd accepted Amanda's offer of a drink. A glass of cold water might help bring down his rapidly rising temperature.

"Answer the question." Blake's steely gaze couldn't be avoided.

However much he tried to look away, Max's eyes were inexorably drawn back. "Yes, I know what a Dom is." Heat bloomed in his cheeks.

Blake nodded. "I thought as much, but I guess your experience is limited to what you've read online?"

Max nodded.

"And you're intrigued. The lifestyle appeals to you."

"I… I don't think we should be talking about this here." Max could hardly believe his own bravery.

"You're absolutely right, Mr. Allenby." Blake steepled his fingers. "So I'll leave you with a proposition to consider over the weekend. It will also give you time to change any plans you may have for next week."

"I don't—" Max clamped his lips shut.

Blake's expression dared him to interrupt again. "From Monday till Friday next week, after work, you will spend

39

three hours in my company, then I'll take you home."

"That's it? Three hours a night for five nights? That's the experiment?" Max didn't feel particularly trusting.

Blake smirked. "Not quite."

"I didn't think so." Max sounded petulant but didn't care.

"During the hours you are with me, you will offer me your complete submission." Blake paused. "You understand what that means, don't you, Max?"

Max squirmed in his chair. He did understand and so did his cock. His body ached with the need to do exactly what Blake wanted, and he had just been given the perfect excuse.

Max nodded and whispered, "Yes, I do."

"Have you had any formal training?" Blake asked.

"Training, Sir?" The use of the honorific suddenly had new meaning. Max couldn't think straight.

"As a submissive." Blake tapped his fingers on the arm of his chair. "Have you ever submitted to a lifestyle Dominant before?"

Max shook his head slowly, hoping that his lack of experience wouldn't disappoint Blake. He seemed to have answered the question in the best possible way, though, because Blake's satisfaction was evident in his smile.

"Excellent. Enjoy your weekend off, Max." He paused. "You won't be seeing anyone in the next two days, will you? Justin said you were single."

*Oh he did, did he?* Max began to imagine all the bad things he was going to do to his big brother in the very near future. He'd had his children—he didn't need his balls anymore. Max shook his head again, not trusting himself to speak.

"Good." Blake's deep voice filled the silence. "I don't share." He gave Max a piercing stare. "I'll expect your answer first thing Monday morning. You may go."

Max stood, praying that his knees wouldn't give way. "Thank you, Sir." He whirled around and made a break for freedom.

# Chapter Four

Lorem Max twirled his spoon in the froth on the top of his triple-shot vanilla latte, destroying the carefully crafted leaf design. "And then I said 'thank you, sir,' and left."

His best friend Cas fell off his stool he was laughing so hard. Max sighed and offered Cas his hand. He hauled him off the floor and Cas retook his seat.

"Let me get this straight." Cas wiped the tears from his cheeks. "Your boss, and I don't mean that bitch in a lab coat, I mean your big boss is gay and he's kinky. He wants to chain you up and fuck you stupid every night for a week and you didn't say yes right there and then?"

Max rolled his eyes. "He didn't want an answer until Monday, Cas, and I didn't say anything about chains. He's a Dominant, a real one. What am I going to do?"

"This is not the kind of conversation we can have perched up here. We need comfy seats, the biggest triple-chocolate muffins I can find and more coffee. A lot more coffee. With *whipped* cream. Dr. Cas will give you all the advice you need. Now go and grab those two armchairs in the back before those women at the counter spot them. Our need is greater."

While Cas scurried away to fetch supplies, Max commandeered the chairs, ignoring the death glare he got from the women queuing for their drinks. "You snooze, you lose," he murmured, dumping Cas' satchel in one chair then sinking into the other. He massaged his temples in an attempt to head off the tension headache building behind his eyes.

"More caffeine is probably a bad idea," Max said as Cas

41

deposited a laden tray on the low table set between their two chairs.

"Hush that blasphemous mouth of yours, the coffee gods might hear you!" Cas pushed a fresh latte and an enormous muffin in Max's direction. "There, now we're all set to discuss your little dilemma, though I'm not sure why you think there's anything to debate. Blake Winters is mega rich, hot as fuck and apparently wants to spank your cute little butt. What's not to like?"

"He's my boss, Cas. Isn't that a relationship train crash waiting to happen? He owns Armacom, for Christ's sake. If this all goes wrong it's not going to be him flipping burgers for a living. And I don't think I mentioned spanking."

Cas took an enormous bite of his muffin then made obscene noises as he chewed. "I think I'm having a chocgasm, is that a thing?"

"I'm sure it is." Max chuckled. Cas always made things better.

"So, is your only issue with dating Blake the fact that he's your big boss?" Crumbs sprayed from Cas' mouth. "Oops, sorry." He swiped the back of his hand across his lips. "Or are you worried that he's going to want to do all kinds of painful things to you?"

"BDSM doesn't have to be about pain, Cas."

"I know that, I'm just teasing."

Max peeled the wrapper from his muffin then broke off a piece. "You've got a lot more experience than I have. What do you think I should do?"

"Are you calling me a slut?" Cas wiggled his eyebrows.

"No! Well, it's true, but no. I want your advice."

Cas poked his tongue out. "Does he make your legs turn to jelly?"

"Um, yes?"

"And does your stomach do flip-flops in his presence?" Max nodded.

"Then physical attraction isn't an issue. The question is, do you trust him?"

"I don't really know him," Max said.

"He wants you to submit to him. That takes a great deal of trust, Max. Would you feel safe if he did decide to tie you up?"

Max chewed on his muffin and gave it some thought. Blake was intimidating, but he'd also demonstrated that he could be caring and attentive. Max's instincts said he could be trusted. Cas took a big slurp of coffee, breaking into his thoughts.

"Yes, I trust him. He wouldn't do anything I didn't consent to, I'm sure of that. Justin adores him, and my brother might be an interfering ass, but he wouldn't work for anyone he didn't trust."

"Then you should say yes," Cas said, as if there were nothing else for Max to worry about.

"But what about the work thing?"

"It's not as if you're sitting in the same room day in, day out. You said yourself that you hardly know him so you obviously don't interact much. If you decide you aren't into him, you'd just go back to the way things were." Cas shrugged. "You're a brilliant scientist, he's not going to fire you if things don't work out between you. It's about time you let yourself have some fun. Of course you'll spill all the juicy details to me after each date night. That's nonnegotiable."

"Cas, I don't ask you about your dates."

"But I tell you anyway!"

"That doesn't mean I have to return the favor."

Cas pouted. "No fair. You're the kinky one. It's your duty to further my education and broaden my horizons."

"You're the one that goes to BDSM clubs, not me!"

"You could come with me, you know. I've asked you often enough. Admit it, you've always fantasized about getting on your knees for some leather-clad Dom."

"Hush!" Max checked out the other customers in case anyone had overheard Cas' comments. "Keep your voice down, you idiot. I don't want the whole world knowing."

Cas sniggered. "It's nothing to be ashamed of, honey."

"I'm not ashamed." Max's denial was a bit too strident. "Am I?"

"Nobody gets to pass judgment on what floats your boat, Max. I'd bet a week's wages half the customers in here have secret sex lives. There's no such thing as normal anymore."

Max sipped his cooling coffee. Despite Cas' reassurances he still wasn't convinced he should say yes to Blake. He wanted to, but that didn't mean he had the courage to go through with it. It might have been easier if Blake hadn't given him time to think about it. He realized that was another reason for saying yes. Blake wasn't forcing him. He hadn't asserted his dominance or put Max in a position where he felt obligated to say yes.

"Why on earth does he want to date a geek like me?"

"Good question." Cas fell about laughing. "For someone with a genius IQ you really aren't very bright, are you? Have you been anywhere near a mirror recently?"

"I'm nothing special," Max said, genuinely confused. "You're the pretty one—all tan and pouty."

"I have a snub nose and freckles. You have this whole quiet, insecure thing going on that attracts men with protective instincts. If you did something with that mop of hair, you'd be almost as pretty as me!"

"What's wrong with my hair?" Max patted his perpetually tangled locks.

"You look like a very pale surfer." Cas pushed his empty mug into the middle of the table. "I think we need to shop, eat lunch then I'll give you some instruction in the art of manscaping."

"You know I hate shopping, Cas. I don't need new clothes... Unless you think I should get something smarter?"

"No, no... He's asked *you* out, not some over-dressed alter-ego. I'm not talking about a new outfit, but you should invest in decent underwear." He winked.

"I have underwear," Max said defensively.

"I should hope so," Cas crowed, "but when did you last

buy anything new?"

"My mom always buys me new shorts for Christmas."

"You *cannot* go on a date with Blake Winters wearing underwear that your mother bought you, much as I love your mom. That's just wrong."

"Fine," Max grouched. "But I'm not putting on anything made of leather or plastic."

"How are we friends?" Cas shook his head. "You are sooo boring."

"And before you think I've forgotten, you are not getting anywhere near my bits with anything sharp."

"Again with the boring."

"I'll let you take me to one store. That's it. No touring half the state like you usually do." Max folded his arms, trying to project his resolve.

Cas mirrored his body language. "I get to choose where we have lunch."

"Fine," Max conceded.

"Fine." Cas giggled.

\* \* \* \*

It was easy to be brave and optimistic in Cas' company, not so much now that Max was home alone in his apartment. He dumped the bags containing his purchases in his closet and decided that unpacking could wait. Needing something to take his mind off Blake, he cleaned his apartment from top to bottom, changed the bed and did the laundry. He sorted through paperwork that had been piling up for weeks and even wrote a shopping list. A trip to the grocery store would take up part of Sunday because he was very aware that he still had another day to fill before seeing Blake again.

All the cleaning was cathartic. He realized that subconsciously he was making a fresh start. Blake had offered him a route to a life he'd been afraid to try. It was past midnight when he tumbled into bed. For a moment, he lay in the dark, enjoying the scent of freshly laundered cotton. Physically he was worn out, but mentally his mind raced like an Olympic sprinter. He tried reciting chemical equations with no effect. Counting test tubes jumping over a fence didn't help either. In the end, he let his thoughts drift where they would. If that made his dreams more exciting then so be it.

* * * *

Max woke in a tangle of sheets, sweating, his breathing ragged. His iron cock taunted him, daring him to touch. The confusion of his dreams faded into vague images of leather and chains, Blake's stormy eyes and the sound of water tumbling over rocks.

"Watersmeet," Max murmured. "Seems like my decision is made." The knowledge gave him a measure of peace and the thrill of anticipation subsumed his anxiety. He took a firm hold of his cock and jerked it rapidly. Without lube there was a slight burn from the friction, which only made him move his hand faster. He spread his legs wider, perspiration slicking his skin.

He closed his eyes and his back arched. He pictured Blake's face and his orgasm crashed over him. Cum coated his hand and splattered his abdomen. He drew a long, shuddering breath. His shaft was so sensitive he couldn't even bear the touch of cotton so he scrambled out of bed then lurched toward the shower.

Half an hour later, clean, dry and dressed in his comfiest sweats, Max lounged on his sofa inhaling a bowl of oatmeal liberally laced with maple syrup. He was scraping the last traces from the bowl when his cell rang.

Max glanced at his watch. "Morning, Cas, early for you, isn't it?"

"Just calling to offer you my support, as any half-decent best friend would do. You know, in case you have any major, life-changing decisions to make today."

Max chuckled. "The decision is made. I'm going to say

yes to Blake. It's only three hours a night for five nights. What could possibly go wrong?"

"That sounds like a line from a bad horror movie just before the first victim heads straight for the mad ax murderer. I'm coming over to save you."

"I don't need saving, Cas." Max smiled. He loved Cas to bits and had no doubt his friend would face any number of psychotic maniacs on his behalf. "I'm planning a day of movies and junk food."

"Last day of freedom, huh?"

Max could hear the plea in Cas' voice. "Something like that. I could handle some company."

"Yay! I mean, let me just check my diary."

"Cas..." Max rolled his eyes.

"Fine, I'm on my way. I'll bring snacks."

"No, I'll meet you at the market. I have a list. Give me half an hour, okay?"

* * * *

By early evening, Max was high on sugar and E-numbers. He lounged at one end of the couch while Cas was laid out with his head in Max's lap. They were coming to the end of a Sharknado movie marathon. Max groped down the side of the couch, searching out his can of soda. It eluded his touch so he twisted his body enough that he could peer over the arm.

"Where's my soda?"

"Drank it," Cas said. "I put the can in your recycling bin." He said that as if it was some kind of defense for his thievery.

"It must be time for pizza."

"With lots of toppings. Anything but fish," Cas said as another shark was blown to bits on the screen.

"Agreed." The titles rolled so Max turned off the set and made a grab for the phone. He put in his order, then shoved Cas off his lap. "Need to go and dunk my head in cold water. I feel all muzzy. Pizza guy said fifteen minutes so haul your lazy ass up and get the door if the delivery arrives before I get back. My wallet is on the table."

Cas grunted, and Max took that as agreement. He sauntered to the bathroom and freshened up a bit. He cleaned his teeth to get rid of the taste of Cheetos and Twinkies mingling on his tongue. "You're a scientist, Max, you should know better than to eat chemically enhanced junk." His reflection was not a pretty sight. One eye was a bit bloodshot, his hair looked like the aftermath of a close encounter with a Van de Graaff generator and his tongue had grown fur. "Gah. Disgusting." He stuck his head under the cold tap and ran the water. "I have to get an early night or Blake is gonna take one look at me tomorrow and withdraw his proposition." He shook his head, scattering droplets everywhere.

"The cheesy goodness has arrived," Cas shouted in his direction when he returned to the lounge.

"I can't believe I'm hungry, but I am."

Cas put the pizza box on the coffee table and levered the lid up. Steam rose from the pie. Max helped himself to a slice, catching strings of melted cheese on his tongue. He took a huge bite. "Mmm, s'good."

Cas didn't reply, he was too busy stuffing his face. They ate in companionable silence until the box was empty. Cas lifted his shirt then rubbed his flat belly. "I must be as fat as a pregnant hippo."

"That's quite the image."

Cas grinned. "Time for some fun. Do you have any beer?"

"No, and you know I can't drink. The only alcohol in the house is a bottle of cognac I bought for Mom last Christmas. She needed it to set the pudding on fire but needless to say I forgot to take it with me. It's been sat in the kitchen cupboard ever since."

"Oh well. I think we can manage truth or dare without lubrication." He giggled. "Though that depends on the dares."

"Oh God," Max moaned. "Cas, I really need to get a decent night's sleep tonight."

"Are you chucking me out?" Cas' bottom lip quivered.

"Casper Collingford, you should be ashamed of yourself. Crying on demand is not going to work."

"It never does with you." Cas pouted.

"I'm not throwing you out. You can sleep over, providing you promise to actually *sleep*, not gossip the night away."

"Cool." Cas was instantly all smiles.

"You're such a faker." Max fetched a couple of bottles of water from the kitchen, then threw one at Cas. "I think we both need some system cleansing, don't you?"

Cas shrugged. "If you say so. This can cleanse the body, truth or dare can cleanse our minds."

"Two goes each, then bed." Max sat down. "I'll take truth first."

Cas sat on the floor, legs crossed. "Okay, if I only get two goes I can't waste them. What aspect of BDSM turns you on the most?"

"How can I answer that if I haven't tried anything yet?"

"From watching it, dummy. I know I'm not the only one who can dig out Internet porn. Come on, you can tell me. The game is as sacrosanct as the confessional."

"Spanking." Max's face heated.

"Giving or receiving? As if I didn't know." Cas giggled.

"That's a second truth, Cas."

"No fair. I claim the right of full disclosure." Cas fluttered his lashes.

"Receiving."

"I knew it!" Cas crowed. "If I could high five myself I would. Okay, I'll take truth as well."

"I'm gonna follow the theme. Have you ever been spanked?"

"Of course! I have a very spankable ass." Cas stretched out on his belly, propping his chin in his hands. "Enjoyed every minute too. My turn."

"Truth again, I don't have the energy for a dare." Max

was having trouble keeping his eyes open.

"If Blake Winters wants to strap you naked to a St. Andrew's cross and whip you, will you let him?"

Max's face grew even hotter. "I don't know… And that's an honest answer, Cas."

"The color of your cheeks tells me you'd give it serious thought." Cas giggled. "I'll take a dare."

Max stood and stretched. "I dare you to spend an entire night in my bed without stealing the duvet."

"No fair, Max! It's not my fault you don't have a guest room."

"There's always the couch." Max headed for the bedroom, fighting back a yawn.

Cas yelped. "No way. The last time I slept on that thing my spine went on strike for a week." He scurried past Max to get to the bed first.

"My bed, my rules."

"Sounds like the kind of thing Blake might say." Cas stripped to his underwear then dived under the covers, giggling.

As he undressed, Max thought about that. How would he respond to another man setting rules for him? He had no idea, but he knew with absolute certainty that he wanted to find out.

# Chapter Five

The clock in the lab had definitely stopped. Max could swear that the hands hadn't moved in hours. Perhaps the damn thing was taking industrial action, some kind of protest against his poor timekeeping? Or maybe Dr. Preston had found a way to slow it down just to keep him slaving away a bit longer. It felt like it had been five minutes to six for the last hour and a half.

Max checked his watch and the digital display in the bottom right hand corner of his computer screen, but they were also part of the plot, telling the same time. It was a conspiracy. He wriggled on his stool and picked up another pencil to sharpen even though it was already so pointy he could probably have used it as a weapon. Now there was a thought – death by pencil. Perhaps he could use it on Justin. His brother had been noticeable by his absence all weekend and Max was now in a very uncomfortable relationship with Justin's voicemail. He'd also made very creative use of emojis in some text messages that could probably get him arrested for threatening behavior.

The long hand hit the twelve with an audible click and Max nearly fell off his stool in shock. It was becoming a habit. Sooner or later he was going to end up on his ass. The interminably long day that had dragged his butt through countless meetings was gone and so was his safety net. He was absolutely terrified, but it was fear generated by excited anticipation, like standing in line for one of those horrifically scary roller coasters, stomach knotted, palms sweaty. He was about to get into the leading carriage and roll over a vertical drop. Nausea had been building since

Blake had rung him that morning—about two minutes after Max arrived at his desk.

"I'll pick you up outside the office tonight at six fifteen." It hadn't been a question, just a statement of fact. Max had been too nervous to be insulted by Blake's presumption. He'd managed a 'yes, Sir' in response and that had been that. No going back.

He powered down his computer then exchanged his lab coat for a black cord jacket with patched elbows. He waved at two colleagues conferring over some paperwork before heading out to the reception area. The night security guard had already replaced the ditzy receptionist behind the front desk but Max didn't know him so he just smiled and left the building.

The cool air outside was a relief and Max took deep gulps, like a drowning man who'd suddenly reached the surface. He didn't normally suffer from claustrophobia but all day it had seemed as if the walls were pressing in on him. He shoved his hands in his pockets in an attempt to stop them shaking. When Blake Winters' sleek BMW drew up at the curb, Max had to force his feet to move from where they'd become superglued to the ground. The tinted window on the driver's side didn't open but when Max reached the passenger door, he realized that Blake was in the driving seat rather than his chauffeur. He got in and fastened his seatbelt.

Max tried not to cringe as Blake gave him an appraising once-over.

"Are you afraid of me, Max?"

Those weren't the first words Max had expected to hear. He shook his head mutely.

"Well, you're doing a damn good impression of someone who is scared rigid. I've seen ghosts with more color."

"I'm a little nervous, Sir." Max couldn't meet Blake's eyes. He was relieved when Blake put the car in gear and pulled away because his gaze would have to be fixed on the road.

"Try to relax. I'm not going to hurt you. This will be a

pleasurable experience for both of us."

"Easier said than done," Max muttered under his breath. Tension permeated every muscle in his body. He closed his eyes and tried to banish the images his mind had been conjuring all weekend in between all the distractions he had tried to create.

The images mainly involved him being naked and chained while Blake, clad in black leather, brandished a variety of whips and floggers. Much as the thought of bondage and pain scared him, his cock seemed to find the whole idea extremely stimulating. Blake had filled his dreams for two nights running. Even sharing a bed with Cas, who not only snored but also talked in his sleep, hadn't prevented that.

"Forget everything you've ever seen on the Internet. I don't have a dungeon in my house."

Blake could, apparently, read minds. Max decided there and then to stop worrying. Blake was gorgeous — spending time with him was hardly punishment. Blake was in charge, therefore decisions were his area of expertise. Max sighed softly and felt the weight lift from his shoulders. A small smile traced across his lips. Blake would tell him what to do and that was how it should be. His world suddenly felt just a little more comfortable, and if Blake was lying, and there really was a dungeon in his basement, so be it.

The rest of the journey passed in silence, though Max sensed Blake glancing across at him several times. The car was warm and comfortable. Max would have been quite happy to travel farther but the familiar crunch of gravel told him that they'd entered the drive to Watersmeet.

"One day I'll bring you here in daylight so you can see the house properly," Blake said. "I'll leave the car here rather than put it in the garage as we'll be going out again later when I take you home."

Max wondered if Blake was trying to make him feel more comfortable by acknowledging that he would be leaving. He followed Blake's lead and got out of the car. He immediately identified the sound of rushing water somewhere in the distance and guessed it might have something to do with the name of the house. Watersmeet seemed romantic to Max, suggesting a tumultuous liaison between natural forces. He kept his fingers crossed that his own evening with Blake would be calmer.

"Why did you choose to build here, Sir?" Max asked.

"Armacom came first. I used to lease a place in Plymouth but once the company was firmly established, I searched around for a plot of land to build on."

"But why this area? I mean, I would have thought Boston or Portland…" Max stopped speaking. It was none of his business. Blake was going to think he was nosy.

"I wanted Armacom to be somewhere quiet, where the staff could have a decent quality of life. I went to Harvard, then worked in Boston for a while, but I prefer less frenetic surroundings. It's easier to concentrate out here. Come, let's get inside."

Soon Max was standing in the spacious hallway of the house. He repressed a shiver as, behind him, the front door shut with a solid clunk. Blake took his jacket and hung it in a closet, then turned and examined him. Max met his gaze for just a moment before his courage failed and he cast his eyes down. He had no time to panic because Blake cupped his face and pulled him forward into a kiss that melted his bones. Blake's lips were so soft as they covered his, his hands warm and strong. Max opened for him willingly, submitting to an insistent, determined exploration. What started gently became rougher as Blake probed deeper with his tongue and nipped at Max's lip. When Blake finally pulled away he kept hold of Max's hair, keeping him in place. He brushed his thumb over Max's mouth.

"That was presumptuous. I should have asked if you kissed, but your mouth was irresistible."

"Oh… I liked it," Max admitted, as much to himself as to Blake.

"That's good, because for the next three hours you belong to me. Every part of your body is now mine, to do with as

54

I please."

Blake didn't ask if he agreed or understood. It was a statement of fact, not a question. Max, still reeling from the most intense kiss he had ever experienced, gave up any pretense of resistance and whispered, "Yes, Sir. Can I... I mean is it okay if I ask a question?"

"Questions are definitely encouraged. Ask away." Blake gripped the nape of his neck.

"Is this a date, or...something else? Having a time limit seems more like a business arrangement."

"It's a date," Blake said with certainty. "The time limit may seem odd but you're inexperienced, Max, and I want you to have some certainty about the evening, and all the other evenings we will spend together this week. It's a small thing, but knowing that our time is finite will ease some of your uncertainty. I don't expect you to trust me instantly, and a relationship that involves Domination and submission takes a huge amount of trust. Handing me power over your body is not to be taken lightly." He leaned in for another kiss.

Max melted against him. Resistance didn't even enter his head. Perhaps if he was really, really good he might be rewarded with more kisses as the evening progressed.

Blake let go of his neck only to wrap his fingers tightly around Max's wrist and tug him toward what proved to be the dining room, housing a beautiful polished maple table and twelve chairs. One chair was set back a little, and on the table in front of it were a shiny pair of handcuffs and a wide strip of black leather. Max's cock jerked hard and he whimpered as Blake maneuvered him toward the chair. He couldn't take his eyes off the items on the table and his heart was pounding.

"Please sit down." The polite request was so much more effective than an abrupt order, but no less insistent.

Max sat. Blake stroked his hair, calming him. Max wanted to push against his touch but kept still—he didn't want to come across as needy.

"Learning to trust begins here," Blake said, his tone gruffer than usual. He picked up the strip of leather from the table and trailed it over one of Max's shoulders. "I'm going to blindfold you, but first we have to agree something important. Do you understand what a safeword is?"

Max concentrated on breathing. There was nothing keeping him in place, and he half-wished there was. He wanted his choices taken away and at that moment he still had the option to bolt. "Yes, Sir. I do." Max felt like he deserved an award for managing to string coherent words together.

"Good. Then you know you need to choose a word that you wouldn't normally use, but that's memorable to you. You'll use it if you want me to stop what I'm doing."

"All I have to do is say one word?" Max knew the principle, he just needed Blake to confirm it. It seemed ridiculously simple.

Blake nodded. "That's right. One word and everything stops. Safe, sane and consensual—those are the watchwords of the BDSM community. Certainly for anyone who presumes to call himself a Dom. A safeword is an unbreakable promise between us. You promise to use it if you need to. I promise to respect it."

Max had the perfect word. "Preston, Sir. Is that okay?"

"For now." Blake grinned. "Not a name you're likely to scream in the throes of passion, is it?"

"God no, Sir." Max managed a giggle—suddenly things were not quite so terrifying. Blake passed the strip of leather around his eyes, blocking out the light. The knot Blake tied pressed hard into the back of his head. The blindfold was tight and immovable. The scent of leather filtered into his nostrils. He had to resist the urge to lift his hands and tug it away. He clenched his fingers into fists and his muscles stiffened. When Blake touched his nape, Max gasped. Then Blake began to knead his shoulders and neck.

"Try to relax." Blake's voice was deep and soothing. "I know this is all new to you, Max, but I promise you will enjoy it. Just let go of the fear."

Max forced his body to loosen and unfurled his fingers. Blake's touch felt so good and when he put aside his panic, he realized that the sensation of strong fingers against his skin was magnified without sight. He sighed.

"Good boy."

The words made Max glow.

There was a clink then cold, unyielding metal encircled Max's left wrist. Blake snapped the cuff shut. Max shivered as Blake pulled his arms behind the chair and fastened his wrists together. Max tugged experimentally on the bindings but they were strong and just dug into his flesh. There was a slight pull on his shoulder muscles but he wasn't too uncomfortable.

"I wish you could see how perfect you look, Max." Blake sounded very close. "So extraordinarily beautiful."

Max's face heated. He spread his knees a little to give his tight balls some breathing space. His cock was rock hard and twitching. He longed to touch himself, but of course that was impossible. Blake now controlled his pleasure as well as his senses. Max grappled with that idea for a few seconds, expecting to be overwhelmed. Instead, the comfort of it sank deep into his bones.

"I'm going to leave the room, Max, just for a couple of minutes," Blake said. "You'll be able to hear me moving around. Are you okay with that?"

Max nodded. He knew Blake would take care of him—that was his job.

"I need a verbal response to my questions, Max." Blake squeezed his shoulder.

"Oh, yes, Sir, I understand. Sorry."

"No need to apologize. I should have been clearer in my instructions. I've taken away your sight. It's important that you know I won't be far away."

Max knew the moment Blake left the room. Even though he couldn't see, Blake had a presence that didn't require sight. His warmth, his scent, the constant touches, the deep, reassuring timbre of his voice all helped Max feel secure. He wondered what Blake was doing. He could hear the clink of crockery and the sound of a refrigerator door opening and closing. The kitchen had to be the next room. Max craned his neck, twisting his head in the direction of the sounds.

The movement of air against his skin told him that Blake had returned and passed close by. Then came the sound of china against wood as Blake presumably placed things on the table.

"How are you doing, Max? The cuffs aren't too tight, are they?"

"No, Sir." Max wouldn't confess it but he loved the sensation of metal against his skin.

Blake lifted Max's hands. "I'm testing your temperature, making sure your circulation isn't compromised. If you experience any tingling or pins and needles, you are to tell me immediately. Handcuffs aren't designed to be comfortable."

"Yes, Sir," Max murmured. A creak told him that Blake had taken a seat next to him. He must have moved another chair. There was a low chuckle then light pressure against his erection. Max held his breath.

"I knew you would respond well to bondage, Max. Do you enjoy being bound for me?"

The pressure went away, and Max remembered how to breathe. He had been seconds away from coming in his pants. He didn't know how to answer Blake's question. He did enjoy it, loved it, but there was no way he was going to admit it.

"No!" The word came out like a sob.

"Liar." Blake sounded so sure of himself, so certain, but there was no anger in his tone. "You're hard and aching. I'm going to keep you on the edge for a long time, Max. Perhaps when you tell me the truth I'll let you come. Not before, though. Not until I say so. Any more lies will be punished. Trust works both ways, after all."

Max whimpered. He longed for Blake's touch. He

wriggled, trying to apply some friction to his needy cock.

"Be still." Blake snapped out the order, and Max instantly froze.

His body reacted even before his mind fully processed the command.

"Now tell me, do you have any food allergies or anything you really hate to eat?"

"I like most things, Sir, but not anchovies or avocado. I'm not keen on anything very spicy. I don't have any allergies."

"Okay. I'm going to feed you. I want you to concentrate on the flavors." The press of something wet against his lips followed.

Max wasn't sure how he felt about being fed like a baby. He tried to jerk his head away from the alien sensation, but Blake grabbed his hair and held him still. "Open."

Reluctantly, Max parted his lips. A burst of flavor landed on his tongue and he closed his mouth around the offered morsel. It slid easily from the fork that speared it. Max chewed and swallowed.

"Wow, that's amazing. Fresh pineapple, I think. It's so moist and sweet." It was delicious and just what his dry mouth needed. His stomach rumbled, betraying the fact that he hadn't eaten all day.

"You really are incapable of looking after yourself, aren't you? Do you ever eat properly?" Blake sounded exasperated.

"I just... I was nervous, Sir. I didn't have much of an appetite." Max ran his tongue along his lower lip, sweeping up the sweet sticky residue. "And I spent yesterday with a friend. We ate far too many unhealthy snacks. And pizza. Oh, and drank lots of soda." Why did he feel an urge to confess?

"A friend?" There was a hint of discontent in Blake's tone.

"My best friend Casper. Cas. It's partly due to him that I'm here with you now. He encouraged me to give this a chance."

"I think I like him," Blake said. "Even if he is a bad

influence on your diet."

"He's a walking trash can when it comes to food."

"Well, from now on it's a rule. You eat a healthy breakfast and lunch. I want to engage in conversation with you, not your rumbling belly." Blake pushed the fork against Max's lips again—this time it held a piece of strawberry.

"Mmm, that's really good." The taste seemed much more pronounced than normal. "I usually have something to eat. I had other things on my mind today." Max tried not to sound too petulant but it was Blake's fault that he had gone hungry. "You're smiling, aren't you?" He pouted, then jerked as Blake brushed a hand across his crotch again.

"Oh dear," Blake murmured. "You and I are going to have a problem, if you come without permission."

"Then stop! Please…"

Of course, begging did no good at all. Blake continued to torture him, alternating between light tormenting touches and firmer rubs. When he finally removed his hand, Max was on the verge of tears. He couldn't remember a time when he'd been so desperate to come.

"I promised to feed you and you distracted me," Blake said, sounding smug. "I think we should get back to the food, don't you?"

"No! I mean… Oh God, I don't know what I mean." Blake had somehow managed to dissolve his brain cells. Max wriggled in a vain attempt to get any kind of pressure on his cock.

"If you don't keep still, I'll tie your legs to the chair," Blake said. His tone was mild but Max knew an order when he heard it. He tensed his thighs in a supreme effort to stop twitching.

"Better."

Max attempted to concentrate on the morsels of food that were pressed against his lips. There were more pieces of fruit, including two different varieties of melon, then small pieces of chicken and fish, cubes of soft bread and herby focaccia with a creamy goats' cheese. Blake took it

60

slowly, asking Max questions between forks. The topics were utterly innocuous, exploring Max's culinary likes and dislikes, favorite restaurants, what he enjoyed cooking himself. Blake ate his share too, Max could hear him. He commented on which foods he liked best as well.

The whole experience was strangely erotic, and Max realized how clever Blake was. Blake had removed his ability to feed himself, something so basic and everyday, yet it allowed him to exert absolute control. The blindfold magnified his senses, making every taste a new experience. Even the small sips of water Max took through a straw tasted fresher.

"Tell me how this makes you feel, Max, and tell me the truth. I'll know if you lie," Blake said. It seemed the meal was done. Blake laid his hand on Max's knee.

Max ducked his head, wondering just how honest to be. He opted for the truth. "I feel owned." He hesitated. "You own my body, my senses... It's scary but exhilarating."

"And do you like the way you feel?"

Max attempted to penetrate the blackness of the blindfold. He desperately wanted to look into Blake's eyes. How could he trust that the man wasn't playing with him if he couldn't see his expression?

"It's hard, isn't it...trusting someone you can't see?"

Blake had to be a mind reader, or maybe Doms had better-honed intuition than most.

"Yes! I do like it." The admission seemed like a failure. Max tugged hard on the handcuffs. "Are you happy now?" A light kiss brushed his lips.

"There's no need to be defensive," Blake said gently. "I'm glad you feel that way, Max, because you *are* mine, and I won't be giving you up at the end of this week."

"Five evenings... That was the agreement!" Though Max protested, a little kernel of hope that Blake might want to keep him set root in his heart.

"Indeed, and I will keep my word. Three hours a night for five nights, then we'll decide what happens next."

61

"I…" Max didn't know what to say. Their first night had to almost be over and he didn't want it to end, but how could he give himself to this man? He hardly knew Blake. Max was a scientist. It made no logical sense to want to *belong* to someone else. It had to be adrenaline, or endorphins, or some kind of chemical reaction. He stopped thinking the moment Blake touched his hair. There was gentle tugging on the knot holding the leather blindfold in place and the pressure around his eyes began to ease.

"Keep your eyes closed at first, Max. I've dimmed the lights but they will still seem bright."

After absolute darkness, even the glow of the light through his lids hurt. Max opened his eyes gradually. He blinked away tears but one stray salty drop rolled down his cheek. Blake stroked it away with the smooth pad of his thumb. Sight increased Max's awareness of other parts of his body. His shoulders ached, his wrists were sore and his cock hurt it was so hard.

"Please let me go, Blake." He peeked shyly through his lashes.

Blake shook his head. "Not yet. I still have half an hour left, I just wanted you to be able to see what I'm going to do next." Blake moved behind him, tilted the chair back and swiveled it around so that it faced away from the table. He remained behind it and leaned over Max's shoulders, running both hands across his chest. Max cried out as Blake simultaneously pinched both nipples through the thin fabric of his shirt, sending a jolt of arousal to his suffering cock. Blake sucked on his neck, no doubt raising a nice, obvious mark, then slid his hands lower until they reached Max's waistband.

"What are you doing…?" Max stuttered as Blake undid his trousers and carefully unzipped his fly.

"I'd have thought that was fairly clear for someone as intelligent as you are, Max." Blake hooked a finger into the elastic of Max's undershorts. "These are very enticing. Are they new?"

"Yes, Sir."

"They cling to you very well. I'm almost jealous." Blake pulled them down just far enough to release Max's straining cock. The band slipped beneath his balls, pushing his genitals forward, displaying them prominently.

Max's face burned and he fought his restraints until Blake placed a hand on his shoulder. "Remember, Max, you promised complete submission. Now stop struggling and behave."

When Blake wrapped his fingers around Max's dick, he sobbed. He was desperate to come, humiliated at being handled in such a way yet so turned on. He was completely at Blake's mercy. Still behind him, Blake played with his cock and balls until Max wanted to scream from frustration. The touches and strokes were light, never enough to bring him off, holding him right on the precipice of orgasm.

"Please! Please, Sir..." he begged shamelessly, trying to thrust into the warmth of Blake's hand.

"You beg very sweetly." Blake circled the base of Max's dick with his fingers and squeezed. "But from this day on you come only when I wish it."

He nipped at Max's earlobe then released his cock. He tangled his fingers into Max's hair and pulled his head back. Max gazed into Blake's eyes and knew he was lost.

"You sadistic bastard!"

Blake smirked and pushed Max's head back down. "I can't deny that your statement is accurate." He flicked the end of Max's leaking cock before tucking him back into his shorts and zipping him up.

Max bit back a yelp as Blake removed the handcuffs and his shoulders gave him a painful reminder of how long they had been pulled back. Blake massaged his shoulders, digging his fingers deep into the muscles.

"Better?"

"Yes, thank you." Max got shakily to his feet and was about to tell Blake exactly what he thought of him when Blake stopped him with a rough kiss. Stubble grazed his

63

cheeks—Blake thrust his tongue deep, and Max forgot that he needed air to survive. His senses were in overload, his mind unable to process the conflicting emotions battering him without mercy. When Blake finally released him, Max no longer recalled why he needed to complain about the way he'd been treated. Blake guided him toward the door, an arm around his shoulders.

"Time's up, Max. I'll be looking forward to our time together tomorrow." There was a hint of amusement in Blake's voice. "I'll drive you home."

Max wanted to snarl something back at him but it was no use—secretly he would be counting the minutes too.

# Chapter Six

Blake stared at the young man curled into the corner of his sofa and allowed himself a smug grin. Even though there was less than six years between them, Max had a boyish appearance that made Blake feel far older. Max was fast asleep, his head resting on the padded arm of the couch. With all signs of worry smoothed from his face, he could have passed for nineteen or twenty, rather than his actual twenty-four years. His tousled blond hair contrasted nicely with chocolate brown leather and fell haphazardly across his face. Dark gold lashes rested against skin the color of pale honey, and a few freckles were scattered across the top of his nose. He had perfect lips—plump and ripe for kissing. Blake licked his own as he recalled doing just that the previous night.

The previous evening had outstripped his expectations in every way. He had dropped Max off at home, given him some instructions for their next date then waited long enough to make sure that he made it inside safely. Max had seemed a bit dazed, his big blue eyes blinking in confusion as Blake had handed him back control of his life. The boy was such a perfect, raw submissive. Blake found it hard to believe that another Dom hadn't already snapped him up, though the thought of another man's hands on Max made his blood boil. He certainly needed protection, and every instinct Blake possessed said he should be the man to provide it. It had been hard to leave him alone for the night. Blake would much rather have tucked him up in his own guest room bed where he could keep a close eye on him.

Max snuffled a little and curled up tighter. He had

changed out of his work clothes and wore a pair of soft jeans, ripped across one thigh, and a charcoal gray T-shirt that proclaimed *Chemists do it periodically* over a picture of the table of elements. He'd left his footwear in the hall closet and his bare feet were tucked half under a cushion. He could be a surfer or postgraduate student—he certainly didn't look like the talented scientist he was. Blake smiled wryly—he should learn not to judge by appearances. Just because he worked hard to maintain the stereotype of a rich, successful businessman that didn't mean Max had to grow a beard and adopt open sandals and socks to fulfill the cartoon image of a science geek.

"Thank God. Time to wake the sleeping beauty," Blake muttered. He wasn't prepared to lose any more of his precious three hours. He touched Max's shoulder gently and placed a steaming mug of coffee on the side table next to him.

"Wake up, sweetheart."

Max's eyes blinked open.

"It's a little distressing that you find my company so soporific."

Max's wrinkled his nose. "It's your fucking fault I'm so tired..." He jerked upright as if realizing what he'd said. "Oh! Sorry, Sir. I was still half asleep." He uncurled his legs and stretched.

Blake drank in the sight of lean muscle flexing as Max's T-shirt lifted enough to reveal a couple of inches of skin. "And how exactly is it my fault that you can't keep your eyes open?"

Max was blushing furiously. "I couldn't sleep, Sir, then Dr. Preston found out that I left work with you yesterday and decided that I needed to spend the day stocktaking in the equipment store."

Blake frowned. Ella Preston would have to be dealt with—he'd been putting off that job for far too long. Max wasn't being paid to count test tubes. "And why couldn't you sleep?" Several emotions warred for control on Max's

66

face.

"You didn't exactly leave me in a condition conducive to a restful night, Sir."

Blake chuckled. "And were you not tempted to give yourself some relief?" He could imagine Max lying there, tangled in his sheets, tossing and turning as he tried desperately not to touch his aching cock. The picture was delicious.

"Of course I was fu — tempted, Sir, but you said — "

"Yes I did," Blake interrupted. "I wasn't sure you would have it in you to obey me, though. I'm impressed."

"I didn't think the alternatives were worth a couple of minutes' relief." Max mumbled the words to himself.

"Don't mutter. I have excellent hearing but I'd rather you spoke clearly. What exactly did you imagine I would do to you?"

"That was the problem, Sir. I started thinking about all the punishments you might come up with. Then every time I closed my eyes..." He shuddered. "It definitely wouldn't have been worth it. Not for the prospect of punishment, because that just keeps me hard, it was the thought of disappointing you that was the real problem. I don't understand why you make me feel this way."

Blake gave him a knowing smile. "Well, perhaps this evening will help clarify things for you. Drink your coffee, Max, I want you to be fully alert for the rest of our time together."

"Yes, Sir. I can make up the lost time if you want me to." He blew on the surface of his drink before sipping.

"That won't be necessary. I allowed you to sleep — it was my decision, not yours. However, I will be maximizing my enjoyment of the time we have left. Come." Blake held out his hand, and Max took hold of it. "You can bring your drink." Blake wrapped Max's slimmer fingers up tight in his own hand and gave him a gentle tug. He steered him through the hall, up the stairs and into the master bedroom. He closed the door firmly.

67

Max didn't hide his curiosity as he gazed around the room. Blake had left the lighting deliberately low but Max couldn't fail to spot the dark blue towels that covered the bed.

"Strip." Blake distracted him with an order. He relieved Max of his mug and placed it on the dresser, careful to put it on a mat.

Max's desire to refuse the command was almost tangible. He stood stiffly, arms at his sides, fingers curling and uncurling. Blake schooled his face into a calm mask. This was what he loved about Max—his innocence, his raw, untested willingness to submit. His internal struggle to understand his own needs was captivating.

"Do I have to tell you again, Max? I prefer not to repeat myself. During our time together your body is mine. You have your safeword. Use it if you need to."

Max shook his head. He began to undress slowly, his hands shaking with nerves.

"Yesterday, I had my hand around your cock. Why so bashful now?" Blake asked. He strolled across to the window and pulled the curtains closed. It was entirely unnecessary—the property wasn't overlooked—but he thought it might give Max more of a sense of security.

Max pulled off his T-shirt and turned to face Blake. His slender body was nicely toned, his skin smooth and unblemished apart from a couple of small, heart-shaped birthmarks above his hip. His shoulder and upper arm still bore the marks of his bike accident, but the bruises were fading to green and yellow, the grazes were all but healed. Blake knew precisely why Max was hesitant and it wasn't just because Blake was still standing there fully dressed.

"The instructions you gave me yesterday, Sir…"

"Are you trying to tell me that you did not obey them?" Blake narrowed his eyes, "Because that would earn you a punishment."

"No! I did… I mean…" Max hung his head, cheeks aflame. "It's embarrassing."

"Preparing yourself for me in the way I require is nothing to be ashamed of, Max. Now please remove the rest of your clothes."

Max unfastened then slid off his jeans. He picked them up, folded them and placed them on the end of the bed with his T-shirt. His silky burgundy shorts clung nicely and did nothing to hide his arousal. He took a deep, shuddering breath and slipped his underwear off in one smooth movement. He placed the garment on the small pile of clothes and faced Blake with eyes that looked like they might spill tears at any moment.

"More new underwear?" Blake asked.

Max nodded. "I have a new pair for every night this week. Cas helped me pick them out. I hate shopping."

Blake enjoyed the little insight. "Then I'll look forward to seeing the rest of the collection. Spread your legs and clasp your hands behind your back."

Max did as he'd been told, gifting Blake with a perfect view of his freshly shaved groin. All the soft, golden curls that Blake had felt beneath his fingers the previous day were gone. Blake couldn't wait to touch and stroke and fondle. He managed to control the urge—he had a plan for the evening and he was going to stick to it, however much his aching cock objected.

"Perfect." And another form of control, though Max wouldn't yet recognize it as such.

The praise brought a slight curve to Max's lips.

"Now, it's time for your reward."

Max raised one eyebrow in question and Blake chuckled. "Yes, Max, you do get rewards as well as punishments. I'm not a total bastard."

Max barely controlled a disbelieving cough, and Blake shook his head. "You do have a long way to go as a submissive, don't you, Max? Now go and lie on the bed, face down."

Max crawled onto the bed in a way that made Blake wonder if the sway of his ass was deliberate. He was going to have to take Max in hand very soon, before he turned into a rebellious little brat.

"Now make a star shape. Arms and legs spread."

As soon as Max had assumed the correct position, Blake circled the bed, pulling out the restraints he had fixed to each corner of the frame. Heavy leather cuffs were attached to short lengths of chain. Soon Blake had fastened each cuff around a slim wrist or ankle, stretching Max's limbs apart and exposing his pretty, puckered hole.

"Lift your hips, boy." Blake adjusted the position of Max's cock and balls so they were not crushed beneath his body. Max moaned at the contact and Blake grinned. He would soon have Max begging for mercy. He stood back and just drank in the sight for a while. Max presented such a beautiful picture, spread and vulnerable. He was trying to twist his head round so Blake went to stand where he could be seen.

"I want you to keep still for me, Max, but you do not have to be silent. You still don't have my permission to come. Understand?"

The slightly wild, desperate look in Max's eyes said that he did understand. Completely.

"Now try to relax. I am not going to leave the room but you may not be able to see me all the time. I will never leave you alone when you are bound for me, Max, okay? I'll always be in the house."

Max whimpered into the pillow and attempted to hump against the sheets.

"That isn't keeping still now, is it?" Blake planted a firm smack across Max's smooth ass and admired the color change of his handprint as the white shape flushed to red.

Max yelped indignantly but his body stilled.

"That's better."

Blake strolled across to the dresser and pressed a button on the Bose sound system sitting on top of it. Waves of classical music filled the room and he sighed happily. He stripped off his clothes down to his underwear then retrieved a bottle of scented massage oil from a drawer. Approaching from the foot of the bed so that Max wouldn't see him, he climbed on and knelt between the boy's spread legs, letting his knees just touch Max's inner thighs. The resulting twitch of muscle was very gratifying.

"Are you naked, Sir?"

"No, Max. I have underwear on."

"Almost naked then."

"Yes."

"That's so unfair!"

"Why's that, sweetheart?" Blake trailed a finger down Max's spine and watched him squirm.

"Because I can't see you!"

"And is that the only problem?" Blake dragged a nail across Max's hole and laughed out loud when his hips bucked in shock.

"Fuck! What are you doing?"

Blake laid one hand on Max's warm ass and stroked him gently. "What do you think I'm doing?"

Max groaned and burrowed his face into the pillow, muffling his words. Blake couldn't make out what he was saying, but from the tension in Max's muscles, he guessed Max assumed he was about to be thoroughly fucked.

Blake smiled wryly—sinking his stiff cock into Max's beautiful ass would be the highlight of his year. However, he knew full well it was too soon. He also suspected that Max might be a virgin, and if that was the case, he wanted Max's first time to be special. There was no question that it was going to be with him. Just not yet, and not while there was any chance that Max might feel compelled.

Blake unscrewed the cap of the bottle of oil and inhaled the heady scent of jasmine. He poured a little oil into one palm then rubbed his hands together until they were slick and warmed. He placed his hands on Max's shoulders and began to smooth the oil into his skin. He worked downward until the slick coating reached the middle of Max's back then began to massage him, digging hard into tense muscles. Max had tied himself in knots. His neck and shoulders were rigid with tension. Gradually, as Blake kneaded and stroked, he felt the stress in Max's muscles melt away. Max began to fully relax. He made sweet little murmuring noises into the pillow that made Blake smile.

"No falling asleep again."

Max grumbled his assent. His skin was silky smooth and Blake intended to touch every inch. He worked his way slowly and deliberately down Max's back, ignored his ass then concentrated on his thighs and calf muscles. He had beautiful legs—lightly dusted with hair, slim but strong—presumably from all that frantic cycling he did when he managed to stay on his bike. Happy that Max was nice and calm, Blake refreshed the oil on his hands and dribbled a little between his ass cheeks, following the shiny rivulet with a finger. He dug his fingers into the muscles and smiled as Max's moans of pleasure grew louder. Making sure his finger was still coated with oil, Blake pressed gently against Max's entrance until the digit was accepted into the tight embrace of his channel.

"That's right, sweetheart, open yourself to me." Blake went no further than the first knuckle of his finger before withdrawing and stroking Max's backside again. "Time to turn over."

Blake clambered off the bed. He wiped his hands on a towel then undid Max's restraints. "Over you go."

Obligingly, Max rolled over and got back into position. He tried to sit up but Blake pushed him down again.

"Patience." Blake swiftly reattached the wrist and ankle cuffs and stepped back to take a look at his victim.

Max was wriggling, trying to get comfortable within the restricted amount of movement he could manage. His smooth cock stood proud from his body, the tip glistening with pre-cum. Blake hunted down a rubber cock ring. He whirled it around on his finger. "Just to prove that I am a kind and generous Master, I'm going to help you resist the urge to orgasm." He stretched the ring over Max's cock and settled it at the base of his balls. Max squeaked and screwed his eyes tightly shut. "Ever used one of these before?"

Max shook his head, eyes still closed.

"Another first then. I hope there will be many more between us. Open your eyes, Max."

Blake took his time oiling his hands again, watching Max's face closely. There was a small crease across his cheek from where it had been pressed into the pillow. His lashes fluttered over eyes that seemed unusually bright.

Blake smiled lazily and shoved his shorts down. He kicked them away, then stood there and enjoyed Max's gaping at him for a minute or two. He wrapped one slick hand around Max's straining cock and the other around his own.

"Holy fuck!" Max's hips jerked, and he yanked on all four restraints simultaneously.

"How does this feel, sweetheart?" Blake moved both hands in tandem, stroking up and down with gentle but firm strokes.

Max's reply was completely incomprehensible. Blake wedged his knees against the side of the bed to give his shaky legs some support and moved his hands faster. His own pleasure was magnified immeasurably by being able to watch Max, bound and helpless, desperately trying to obey the command not to come. Max had given up any attempt to keep still and was thrashing as much as the short chains holding him down would allow, his skin slick with perspiration. Blake's orgasm built, the slow burn increasing to a fiery need for release. He let go of Max's cock and focused on his own—within a few strokes he came, spattering Max's belly with creamy ribbons of cum.

"No! You bastard!" Max wailed his frustration.

Blake took a few ragged breaths then leaned over and kissed him. "You weren't allowed to come, Max, remember?"

"Oh God, I think I hate you. You can't leave me like this for another day, you just can't!"

73

"Oh, I think I can." Blake strolled into the en suite, cleaned himself up then returned to the bedside with a wet washcloth. He gently wiped Max's body, watching with amusement as his cock jerked and twitched. He released the restraints and checked for any damage to Max's skin.

Max wound his fingers into the towel beneath him and squeezed his eyes shut.

Blake looked down at him, content that he'd brought him to such a state. "I'll give you a choice, Max. You can touch yourself now and accept punishment tomorrow, or you can go and take a nice, cold shower."

If looks could kill, Blake decided that he would be very, very dead.

"Fuck you!" All the previous night's resolve evaporated. Max tore off the cock ring, gripped his dick and tugged frantically. It only took a few seconds before he spurted his release and Blake had to employ his cloth again.

While Max lay panting, Blake pulled on his clothes. He felt warm and satisfied. His plans for the evening had worked out perfectly and now he could look forward to teaching his less than willing submissive something about discipline.

"Was it worth it?"

Max sat up. He drew his knees up and wrapped his arms around them. "Definitely."

"Are you sure? A moment's defiance, a brief release in exchange for what? You don't even know the price." Blake passed Max his clothes.

"So, you're going to punish me. How bad can it be?" Max's voice tailed off.

Blake didn't answer, he just smiled.

"Wait, you're not going to tell me?" Max sounded much less sure of himself.

"My time is up, Max. Get dressed, then I'll take you home. You'll have to wait until tomorrow evening to discover my intentions."

Max scrambled into his clothes. When he was done, he

stood by the bed, hands on hips. "You planned this all along, didn't you? You knew I wouldn't be able to stop myself."

"If I did, I'd hardly confess it." It hadn't taken Max long to work it out. Blake was pleased. He wanted Max to spend the next day wondering what was going to happen—if he'd made a mistake by taking the easy option. He needed to learn that obedience was by far the smoother path. "There are many ways to teach control, Max. Your lessons have only just started."

"You only have three days left, maybe I'm a slow learner."

"We both know that's not true." Blake chuckled. "Let your analytical mind get to work, Max. It won't help. Try exploring your feelings instead. What is it you truly want? Does rebellion make you feel good? I don't think it does. You want to please me, want to submit—but it isn't easy. The effort you put in will be worth it in the end, that's a promise I can safely make."

Max frowned. "I definitely hate you just a little bit."

"Excellent. We're off to a fine start."

* * * *

Max lay in bed staring at the ceiling. He was naked, the covers kicked down to his feet. His erection refused to subside and he had a death grip on the sheets to stop himself from touching.

"Surely I can summon up willpower from somewhere!" Max shouted. He'd given in to the physical demands of his body earlier that evening, thinking he could deal with the prospect of Blake's punishment. But now he regretted his weakness. Blake had given him a choice but the knowledge that Blake had assumed he would fail knotted Max's stomach.

Giving up on the idea of sleep, Max grabbed the phone and dialed Cas' number.

"I'm not speaking to you."

Cas had caller ID. Max sighed, making sure it was loud enough for Cas to hear.

"Seriously, I am your ex best friend right now."

"What did I do?" Max had a pretty good idea why Cas had a stick up his ass.

"You're the one with the ginormous brain. Work it out."

"Cas..." Max pleaded. "I'm sorry, okay? I should have called you sooner."

"One measly apology is not going to cut it. I can't believe you've spent two nights with Mister Hot and Gorgeous and I haven't heard a single kinky detail. Call yourself a friend?"

Max let Cas carry on berating him for a few minutes. Cas needed to get it out of his system. He finally subsided into silence.

"Are you done?" Max chuckled.

"I could go for round two," Cas sniped. "But I'd rather you dished the dirt. Tell me everything. Right now."

"If I could get a word in, I would."

"Max, if you don't start talking I'm coming over there. I've had two cans of Red Bull, so believe me when I say it won't be pretty."

"I'm already in bed. Can't sleep. The last two days have been...intense."

"Are you okay? Blake didn't hurt you, did he? If he did something to you, I will hunt him down and snark him to death, I promise."

"He didn't hurt me, Cas, far from it. He's just so... I don't know."

"So dominant? Overwhelming? Tantalizing?"

"All of those things. I can't really explain. He has this aura..."

"What, one of those glowy light halo thingies?"

"No, Cas. Not one of those. And where did you get that from anyway?"

"I read graphic novels. Stop trying to change the subject."

"I wasn't..." Max got out of bed. He paced up and down,

gripping the phone so hard his knuckles went white. His frustration wasn't with Cas—it was with the way Blake made him feel. "He makes me want to please him." There, he'd gotten the words out. The silence on the other end of the line was a little disconcerting. "Cas... Are you still there?"

"I'm here." Cas' voice broke.

"Hey, are you crying? I didn't mean to upset you, Cas."

"It's just soooo romantic, I can't help myself. You've fallen for him, haven't you?"

Relieved, Max smiled. "I suppose I have."

"Well then, what's the problem?"

Max realized that he was beginning to feel chilled. He clambered back into bed and pulled the covers up. "I suppose it's because everything is happening so fast. We've spent a total of less than seven hours in each other's company."

"Ah, but you've been crushing on him for almost two years. It's not like you met in some bar as strangers and got straight down to it. Not that I'm saying there's anything wrong in that of course. In fact, it has its advantages... Sorry. I'm rambling."

"It still wasn't real until this week." Max thumped his pillow into a new shape. A feather lifted into the air on a puff of wind then floated to the carpet. Max watched it fall, admiring the gentle glide to earth. "He called it a trial, Cas. What happens at the end of the week when he gets bored of me?"

Cas snorted. "Don't be ridiculous. He's not going to get bored of you. He's going to great pains to make sure you're comfortable with him. That doesn't seem like a short-term thing to me."

"He could have anyone, Cas. Why has he chosen me?"

"Wow, you really need some self-esteem coaching, don't you? He looks at you and sees what he likes. What he needs."

"He doesn't need me." Max was very much afraid that

the opposite was true regarding his own desire for Blake.

"What makes you think that his side of the equation is any different from yours? If he's a Dom, he needs a sub. Seems pretty simple to me."

Max let that play over in his mind for a bit. Cas' logic made sense. His scientific brain responded to the idea of co-dependence. "It's a chemical reaction. We need *each other*. It's no different from covalent bonding."

"Riiiight. Whatever makes you happy."

Max heard the snap of a ring pull followed by a fizzing sound. "Are you having a third can of that rocket fuel?"

"Uh-huh. I have the day off tomorrow so there's an all night movie marathon in my immediate future. I have a date with Han Solo. You're welcome to come join me."

"I'll pass. I *do* have to work tomorrow."

"Okay. Well, you're officially reinstalled as my best friend. Call me soon or I will hunt you down."

Cas rang off before Max could say anything else. He relaxed against his pillows and smiled into the darkness. Maybe now he would sleep.

# Chapter Seven

Max paced up and down the pavement outside his apartment block. He checked his watch for the hundredth time. When Blake's email had popped up on his computer earlier that afternoon he'd taken it as a brief reprieve. Blake had been called to an important meeting in Boston and would not return until the evening. He'd arranged to pick Max up from home at eight. Instead of enjoying a couple more hours of freedom, Max had found himself itching to be in Blake's company again.

"What the hell is wrong with me? I should be dreading this evening, not looking forward to it." Max didn't care that his neighbors might spot him talking to himself — they already had him pegged as a mad scientist. He couldn't do his reputation any more harm with a bit of muttering. "God, what is he going to do to me?" His cock, already hard, rose in anticipation. Max slapped at his groin. "This is all your fucking fault, you're going to get me into even more trouble!"

"Sign of madness, you know."

Max whirled around. He hadn't heard Blake's car draw up, or the hiss of his window sliding down. Too busy listening to the sound of his own voice. Now Blake peered from the car, chuckling.

"What is?" Max walked around the car and got in.

"Talking to yourself." Blake checked his mirrors and did a neat U-turn so that he was on the correct side of the street. "What were you doing, giving yourself your own personal pep rally?"

"Something like that." Max clicked his seatbelt closed,

praying that Blake hadn't heard him conversing with his own body parts.

"As it's my fault that we are starting later tonight, I'll include travel time in our three hours," Blake said.

"But that will only leave us two hours!" Max exclaimed before his brain connected with his mouth. He shouldn't have revealed his disappointment.

"And that distresses you?" Blake smiled as if that gave him inordinate pleasure.

"I... No, of course not. I don't want you to think you've been short-changed, that's all."

"Oh, don't worry. I'll be getting plenty of value out of you tonight." Blake switched on the CD player and hummed along to the music.

"The prospect of administering punishment puts you in a good mood then?"

"Since you ask, yes. It does. The anticipation of our time together this evening has improved my entire day." Blake drummed his fingers on the steering wheel.

"Glad I could be of service," Max sniped.

"Service suits you. You like to feel needed."

Max turned that thought over in his head. Blake was a bit too perceptive. He did get satisfaction from pleasing others, it was true, but pleasing Blake wasn't just satisfying, it was becoming essential. Max didn't want Blake to be upset with him. Ever.

"I'm sorry, Sir. About yesterday. I should have had better self-control."

"I know you are. You'll take your punishment and wipe the slate clean. It will be a lesson learned and you won't do it again, will you?"

"I'm not sure I can make that promise, Sir."

Blake laughed. "No, I don't suppose you can, but you'll learn that discipline is an integral part of a D/s relationship. I'm introducing a new rule from tonight. No swearing. Each time you transgress, a point will be added to your tally. Eventually, that will be converted to strokes from the instrument of my choice."

"Fuck!"

"That's one." Blake sounded unbearably smug.

Max couldn't come up with a suitable retort or defense. He slumped in his seat, retreating into his thoughts. He wasn't a pain-seeking masochist, he was a grown man, so why did the idea of Blake disciplining him have so much erotic appeal?

*None of this makes any logical sense. I must be losing my mind.*

"This isn't something you can reason out by thinking, Max." Blake turned into the drive to Watersmeet. "It has nothing to do with intelligence, or the lack of it. It's everything to do with your nature, the way you were born. You don't question the fact that you're gay, do you?" He turned off the ignition. The sudden silence was overwhelming, and Max longed for the white noise of the engine.

"Of course not."

"Being submissive is no different. Submission is a gift, Max. A wonderful gift from sub to Master, and believe me, I feel very privileged that you trust me enough to offer yours."

"But you're so...sure." Max's lower lip quivered.

"A Dominant is nothing without a submissive to complete him. Believe me, Max, I need you as much as you need me."

It sounded so much like Cas' words from the previous night. Max had to acknowledge that his friend might have been right.

Blake got out of the car. He walked around it then opened Max's door. He offered him his hand. The moment Max took it, his fears faded. He held tight all the way into the house. The hall smelled of beeswax—it was comforting and reminded Max of his parents' place. His mom didn't believe in newfangled sprays.

"A dollop of wax and some elbow grease."

"Excuse me?" Blake said.

"My mom uses proper polish too. That's what she always used to say." He inhaled deeply. "The beeswax—it has a

81

very distinct smell."

Blake shook his head. "I thought you were proposing some new kind of lube."

Max choked back a laugh. "No, Sir."

"How about I give you the fifty cent tour?"

"I'd love to see the rest of your home, Sir." Max thought he might get a bit more insight into Blake's character, as he had designed the house himself. He was also curious. Watersmeet was special to Blake, more than bricks and mortar, and Max wanted to know why.

"Very well, take your clothes off please."

"You're always so polite, even when you're ordering me around," Max said. He stripped, folding each garment as he went, placing them on the hall table. He slipped his sandals beneath it. For once his nudity didn't make him blush.

"Good manners cost nothing," Blake said, sliding his belt from its loops. "An order is an order, shouting doesn't make it any more so."

Max wondered if Blake was going to get naked too. His cock, already firmly erect, jerked at the prospect. Blake threaded the end of the belt through the buckle, making a small loop. He placed the loop over Max's rigid shaft and pulled it tight.

"You'll need to maintain a steady distance behind me to keep this taut. If it slips off, you'll be punished." Blake gave his makeshift lead a tug.

"Oh God." Max, certain that his entire body must now be bright pink, kept pace with Blake as he strolled down the hall. It wasn't quite how Max had envisioned being introduced to Blake's home. He tried to take in everything Blake told him about the design, its influences and all the arguments he'd had with his architect in order to make everything perfect. He attempted to be enthused by paint effects, designer wallpapers and gleaming wood. It was impossible. Blake acted as if it were perfectly normal to tow a naked man around by his cock. He kept up a running commentary from the lounge to the snug to the stunning indoor swimming pool and gym, but Max's entire world had become determined by the length of Blake's belt.

"I'll show you the grounds another time," Blake said. "It's a little brisk out there tonight." He kept walking, his pace slow enough that Max was in no danger of falling behind.

Max followed him back to the snug where Blake finally released Max's aching dick. His relief lasted scant seconds before Blake wrapped the belt around his wrists, strapping them together so that his hands rested on his belly. A shiver ran the length of Max's spine. The belt wasn't tightly knotted—he could get free if he wanted to—but he was gradually coming to realize that wasn't the point. Blake had placed him in bondage, so he would stay that way until Blake freed him. The knowledge was calming. He relaxed his shoulders and waited for Blake to speak.

"I think I've kept you waiting for your punishment long enough. It's time I dealt with yesterday's infraction."

"Yes, Sir." Max checked the walls for chains. He didn't spot a whip or anything similar on the bookshelves. The mantle over the fireplace held a vase of white roses—there was no sign of a flogger or paddle. He shuffled his feet, wondering how much he would be able to take before he broke.

"Put whatever you are imagining out of your head," Blake said. "Light the fire, please—it's laid ready. All you have to do is strike a match."

Max knelt in front of the hearth, his movement as graceful as he could make it with his hands bound. He pushed open the matchbox, hands shaking. A few matches scattered around his knees.

"Sorry!" He tried to scoop them up but the annoying little sticks kept getting away from him.

"Calm down." Blake knelt next to him, placing his hand on Max's bare thigh.

Max froze. Blake's hand was far too close to his rigid cock for him to concentrate on anything else. Serenity was getting further and further from his grasp. The scrape of the

83

match against the striking strip seemed unnaturally loud. Max was relieved when the crackle of flames shattered the silence. The heat bathed his skin, flickering shadows lighting the room in a golden glow. He stared into the fire, willing Blake to touch him again. He would readily beg if he thought it would do any good.

"Position yourself face down over the footstool." Blake's deep growl broke into Max's thoughts. "Arms out in front of you."

The piece of furniture Blake referred to was a cube of padded leather about three feet square set in front of two armchairs facing the fire. Max began to rise.

"No. On your knees."

Max hoped that his burning cheeks could be put down to the fire. He crawled the few feet to the stool, then lay across it. It supported him from chest to hips but his head hung off one edge, his ass off the other. He was too high up for his knees to reach the ground so he braced his legs and dug his toes into the carpet. It wasn't in any way dignified. To add to his humiliation, and apparently his arousal if his aching balls were anything to go by, Blake patted his backside as he walked past.

"Very good. Spread your legs a little wider."

Max wished his hair were longer, then he could have hidden behind it. Not that he would have felt any less exposed.

"I've warmed this up a bit, but it will probably still seem cold."

"Holy fuck!" Max attempted to scramble off the footstool but pressure on the small of his back kept him in place. From the weight and grip at the base of his balls, Max knew he was now adorned with a heavy-duty cock ring. The chilly metal soon heated against his skin but the pressure was intense, much stronger than the rubber ring Blake had used before. Any small chance he had of coming that evening instantly disappeared.

"That's two."

Max groaned.

"Have you heard of milking?" Blake asked. Warm oil dribbled between Max's cheeks.

"I'm a scientist, Blake, I know where cow juice comes from."

Blake chuckled and began to massage the oil into Max's skin, rubbing the edge of his hole until his muscles twitched. "Wrong kind of milking, sweetheart. It's possible to milk a man too."

Max took a while to catch on. Blake was fingering his hole and it was all he could do not to scream. "You mean...? No! You wouldn't do that to me, Sir."

"Punishment, Max. Remember. You aren't able to orgasm but you're going to want to, very much. The process can take anything from ten minutes to an hour. I'm going to milk you dry, then take you home frustrated and wanting."

"No! Sir... Spank me, flog me, anything but this."

"If you knew how appealing I find your protests, you'd keep quiet."

Max whimpered.

"I want you to keep still. No squirming. You aren't tied down—I want you to stay where you are by my will alone. Do you understand, Max? You will gift me your body to punish as I see fit."

Max bit the inside of his cheek in an effort to prevent himself swearing. He was so turned on and he hated feeling that way. He should be making a run for it, not anticipating Blake's touch with every atom of his being.

When it came, the pressure of Blake's finger inside him made his cock tingle. He didn't understand how it worked, but it did. The gentle pressure on his prostate was relentless. In seconds, Max couldn't think. His vision blurred. He hovered on the edge of intense pleasure that never materialized. The unremitting torment took away all his sense of time. He was vaguely aware of fluid leaking from his cock because Blake would rub it into his shaft at intervals and the scent of his cum filled the air. There was no stretch or burn. Blake used a single finger, rubbing in steady circular motions. Every time Max sobbed and clenched his channel around the invader, Blake would simply pause, wait for him to relax, then begin the torture again.

Finally, after what seemed like hours, Blake withdrew his finger. He removed the cock ring first. There was a rustle of tissues as he cleaned Max up, then warmth and comfort as he gathered him into his arms. Blake undid the belt from his wrists and held him close, planting light kisses on his neck and shoulder.

"It's over, sweetheart. You took your punishment well."

Max leaned against him, trying to get as close as possible. Blake's erection pressed against his belly. "Sir, you're hard!"

"Well of course I am," Blake chuckled. "I've just had the pleasure of playing with your adorable ass."

Max wriggled until Blake released him. He dropped to his knees and nuzzled Blake's crotch. "Please, Sir?" He peeked up at Blake through his lashes.

"Time's up, Max. I should take you home." Blake ruffled his hair.

Max pouted. He didn't move.

"But you were very good this evening..."

Euphoria flooded Max's system. He tackled the button and zip blocking his goal, then pulled Blake's pants down to his hips. He mouthed Blake's cock through the cotton of his underwear before pulling his white briefs down. Blake's dick sprang free, hitting Max's face. He caught the bobbing tip in his mouth and lapped up the drop of pre-cum welling in his slit. Blake smelled and tasted delicious.

"Yes, Max!" Blake's voice cracked.

Max hummed happily. He wanted to be responsible for Blake coming apart. He needed to prove that beneath the stern exterior, Blake had some vulnerability. He licked the length of Blake's shaft, enjoying the thick-ridged vein on the underside. He mouthed Blake's balls, giving each plenty of attention.

Blake grabbed his hair, holding him in place. Evidently it

was impossible for him to give up control completely. Max opened his mouth wide and kept still while Blake thrust toward his throat. His jaw ached. Blake's cock had an ample girth that was challenging to take.

"That's it. Take me," Blake muttered, his voice rough as gravel.

If his mouth hadn't been stuffed full, Max would have indicated his willingness. As it was, all he could do was attempt to control his gag reflex while Blake fucked his mouth.

"I'm close," Blake gasped.

Max resisted Blake's tug on his hair. He sucked hard. When Blake came and liquid heat coated his throat, Max swallowed every drop. Blake let his softening cock slip from between Max's lips. He took a shuddering breath.

"Thank you, sweetheart. That was…astounding."

"Believe me, Sir, it was my pleasure."

Max helped him adjust his clothing, then Blake collapsed into one of the armchairs, pulling Max into his lap. Max buried his head in the crook of Blake's arm. He just wanted to be held, to know that Blake had forgiven him completely. Their time together that evening was almost at an end and Max knew that he would soon have to go home. The thought scared him. He was already becoming reliant on Blake's control, his care—and that was the most terrifying thing of all.

# Chapter Eight

"What do you mean he's not in?" Blake asked his personal assistant impatiently.

Amanda Cross stared at him with an obviously calculated amount of scorn. "I think I was perfectly clear, Mr. Winters. Max Allenby is not here, he phoned in sick this morning. That's what Dr. Preston told me when I called her not ten minutes ago."

"Sick with what? What's the matter with him?" Blake tried to sound calm but wasn't making a very good job of it. Agitation made him snappy and impatient.

"I didn't probe for details because all you asked me to do was to get him over here for a meeting. Would you like me to investigate further? There's no requirement for a staff member to provide information on the nature of their illness, you know. Procedure is just to inform your line manager. Dr. Preston may not know anything more." Amanda's small smile said that she knew exactly why he was so interested but she was too professional to admit it.

"I signed off the procedure, remember? I know the rules. But yes, see what you can find out. No, wait. I... Can you get me his address?" He employed his most beseeching expression. "Oh, and ask someone to bring my car round... I'll be going out."

"Sam is still on holiday. I can call for a replacement driver."

"No, I'll drive myself." Blake paced back and forth in front of his assistant's desk.

"And I suppose you'll be wanting me to reschedule today's appointments?" she asked, hands on hips.

Blake attempted to look a little bit sheepish. "That would be very helpful, Amanda. Thank you." He made a mental note to order her some flowers.

"And what reason should I give if I'm asked?" She grinned, clearly enjoying herself. Blake downgraded the bouquet.

"Make something up." He grabbed his jacket.

"He's very sweet, Blake. Don't scare him." Amanda rarely used his Christian name in the office, so he paid attention despite his desire to get to Max as quickly as possible.

"You approve then?"

She nodded. "I do, he's perfect for you. So if you can hang on for fifteen minutes or so, I'll sort out a care package for you to take with you."

Within half an hour, Blake was on the road armed with an address and a box stuffed with sandwiches and muffins, courtesy of Amanda. He used his hands-free car phone to call Max again but only got voicemail in response. He couldn't help but worry. In just a few short days Max had become much more than a project or experiment. The young scientist had wormed his way into Blake's affections with his sweet, shy nature and hints of brattish resistance. He was the perfect submissive, or would be with a little careful molding.

"I should never have let him out of my sight," Blake muttered as he drove. "He needs constant supervision, I swear. How can he be ill? He was perfectly fine when I dropped him off last night." Niggling doubts crept into Blake's mind. Had he been too harsh? The previous evening had been intense for both of them. Was Max's absence just an excuse to avoid their last two evenings together? *I don't care if he's contracted bubonic plague – he agreed to another six hours.* Blake drove a little faster.

Max's apartment was in a relatively modern, wood-clad block on a quiet estate. The area was neat and tidy with plenty of green spaces, if a little uniform for Blake's taste. He parked the car in a small lot set aside for visitors, found

89

the entrance to the correct block and climbed four flights of stairs to the top floor because he didn't have the patience to wait for the elevator. There were only two doors on either side of a narrow landing. Blake turned left and pressed the bell next to 4A.

He adjusted his grip on the box of food and tapped his foot impatiently for a few seconds before pressing the bell again. After another minute, he knocked firmly. He was contemplating the possibility of finding the nearest fire ax or kicking the door in when he heard shuffling and grumbling behind it. The door opened and Blake couldn't help but smirk at the expression of utter shock on Max's face.

"Oh my God. What in the name of all that's holy are you doing here?" Max's face was chalk white, tinged with green.

"Sir." Blake stated firmly.

Max just looked confused.

"It's what the hell are you doing here, *Sir*?" Blake didn't wait to be invited in. He strolled straight past Max into a narrow hallway and kept going until he reached a compact kitchen diner. He set his box on the counter then turned around to make a more thorough examination of his sub.

"What on earth have you done to yourself?" Blake took in the crumpled shorts and T-shirt that Max had clearly been sleeping in. His hair stuck up wildly in all directions. There were dark shadows beneath his eyes and tiny frown lines betrayed a headache.

"Why do you care?" Max didn't make eye contact—he ducked his head and seemed to be studying his own bare feet.

"Speak to me with respect, boy, or I'll take you over my knee right now." Blake kept his tone mild but still projected absolute certainty. If ever a sub was in need of a good spanking, it was Max.

Max shuffled his feet. "Not a boy. Sorry...Sir." He didn't seem to have any idea what to do or say next so Blake did what he did best and took charge.

90

He left Max standing in the kitchen and went to find the bathroom. He turned the shower on to heat up, made sure there were towels ready then went to fetch Max. He took Max's wrist and led him gently but firmly along to the bathroom. Once there, he unceremoniously stripped him bare.

"Boy is a term of endearment, not an insult. Get in the shower. Now."

Max sighed but stepped beneath the spray. His lower lip jutted just a little. Not quite enough to qualify as a pout, but close.

Blake lounged against the sink while Max soaped his body then shampooed his hair silently. Even through the steamed glass of the cubicle, Blake could make out Max's swollen cock. He had a beautiful body and Blake realized there and then that he never wanted anyone else to set eyes on it. Max was his.

The shower stopped and Max stepped out, skin glistening, scattering shiny droplets as he moved. Blake handed him a towel. "You've got fifteen minutes to get dry, shave, clean your teeth and dress. I'll be in the kitchen."

"You can't order me around here, Blake, that isn't part of the deal. This is my home, not yours." Max's attempt to sound defiant was ruined by the slight tremble in his voice.

Blake scowled, grabbed the edge of Max's towel and yanked it away. He spun him around and landed a couple of hard slaps across his damp backside. "Do as you're told or there will be a lot more of those." He grinned as Max's cock jerked excitedly. "Or perhaps that's what you really want?" He didn't wait for an answer. A dripping, naked Max was far too much temptation. He threw the towel on the floor and stalked out, pointedly leaving the door wide open.

Fifteen minutes later, a slightly flushed Max arrived in the kitchen wearing a pair of faded jeans and a long-sleeved black T-shirt. The fabric clung to his slender form and Blake could hardly tear his gaze away. He sat at Max's breakfast bar sipping coffee made in a cafetière he'd discovered standing on the worktop. He pushed a glass of orange juice and a wholemeal muffin toward Max. "Sit down and eat. You need something in your stomach."

Max pulled a stool over then sat down a little gingerly. He took a sip of the juice.

"Now, can you tell me why someone who can't drink worth a damn has the mother of all hangovers?" Blake held his mug up in a toast.

Max chewed a small piece of muffin before looking up. "How do you know I'm not sick?"

"It's a fairly easy deduction, genius. You were absolutely fine last night, no sniffles or other symptoms, and now... Well, I suspect you have a nasty headache and you look like you didn't get much sleep, probably because you spent half the night throwing up. What's going on, Max?"

"It's all your fault." Max whispered the words as if saying them hurt.

Blake took another sip of coffee and waited for more.

"Last night... What you did to me... I was so confused. I couldn't sleep, couldn't think... Every time I thought about lying over that fucking stool, I got hard, so I jacked off. Twice. Then I started to worry about what you would do to me when you found out because I knew you *would* find out. So I had a drink. Just to relax. There was a bottle of brandy in the cupboard that I forgot to give my mom during the holidays. She didn't need it afterwards so it just sat there. But it didn't help, so I had another and... Then I lost count. I think I passed out for a while and when I woke up I was so sick." He glared at Blake. "Why do you make me feel this way? I should hate you, but I don't. I hate being away from you, it's crazy! What you did last night was torture. What's wrong with me...?"

"Why do you think there's something wrong with you?" Blake raised a curious eyebrow.

"I'm a grown man. It's not right to enjoy being controlled by someone else."

92

"You're a submissive, sweetheart, it's your nature. That doesn't make you any less of a man. It doesn't mean you're weak or even insecure. It just means that you enjoy the peace and calm that comes from handing power to someone else."

"Not *someone* else. You. I've never felt this way before, Blake, not so deeply. I want you to give me orders, tie me up, punish me... Oh Jesus, what am I saying?" He moaned. "I want you to be pleased with me, and I keep failing."

Blake fought to keep control of his emotions. Max's words sent a joyful thrill through his entire body. He wanted to pull Max into his lap and cuddle all the doubts and fears away but he knew it wasn't that easy.

"I think it's time to make a change to our little arrangement, Max."

Max shivered and his blue eyes glistened. "You don't want me? I knew it."

Blake shook his head. "Don't make unqualified assumptions. That's not it at all. I don't want you for three measly hours a night. I want you to be mine. All the time."

"Be yours? You mean be your...submissive?"

"Yes, Max, that's what I mean, though you don't need to put a label on it. I want a partner. A boyfriend."

"But you're a Dominant."

"And it's part of me just as much as submission is part of you. Domination doesn't mean dictatorship, Max. You need to give up control. I need to take it, but nothing happens without your consent. Nothing. In a relationship, we'll be equal partners, just with different needs. I'm a man just like you."

"Really?" The beginnings of a smile flickered around Max's lips.

"Really." Blake stood up. "Finish your juice, I'm taking you back to my place." He gestured at the carton of food. "We can take Amanda's treats with us for later when your stomach is a bit more settled."

"Amanda sent all this?"

Blake chuckled. "I understand your skepticism, but yes. My hardass assistant apparently has a soft spot for you. As do I."

Max looked completely shell-shocked but he swallowed the last of his drink, ate the final scraps of muffin then rinsed his crockery. "Should I pack anything? Clothes, or…"

"You'll come with me then?" Warm satisfaction seeped through Blake's bones.

Max nodded. "I can't not. Does that make any sense?"

"It does. We had two evenings left—we'll just run them together. Then it's the weekend and your time is your own. I hope you will choose to spend it with me. Don't concern yourself with packing more than a few basics. I have toiletries at home and you won't be needing too many clothes." Blake's smile was feral. He had every intention of immersing Max in submission for the next forty-eight hours. The shock would either send him running for the hills or confirm that it was exactly what he needed.

While Max packed a small overnight bag and hunted down his shoes and a jacket, Blake called the office and spoke to Amanda, who immediately enquired after Max.

"Is he okay? Tell me you were kind to him."

"Yes, he's fine, but he needs today and tomorrow off. Can you let Ella Preston know that he'll be back in the lab next week please? I'll be working from home. I'll call you later to rearrange my schedule for the rest of the day."

"I've already canceled your meetings and sent the most urgent business to your inbox. It won't hurt for you to take a few hours off either."

"Amanda, you're a star. If I get through enough today I would like to take Friday off, but I'll see how it goes. I'll talk to you in a couple of hours." He hung up and turned into Max's curious gaze. "Ready? Is there anyone you need to tell that you're going to be away for a few days?"

"No, I have my phone. I can text Cas. Justin will probably check up on me once he finds out I'm off sick. He's worse than my mom."

94

"He'd make a great Dom."

"Nah. He's a pussycat compared to you. Have you ever met his wife? My sister-in-law wears the pants in that relationship regardless of anything my big brother might say." Max picked up his keys and played with them. He looked exhausted, uncertain and a little lost.

Blake took a firm hold of his wrist and immediately felt him relax. Max was so obviously in need of a caring Master.

"How have you not been scooped up by some other man before now?" Blake stroked Max's inner arm with his thumb.

"I don't have much of a social life. I don't do well in crowds and if a guy ever speaks to me I just stutter then clam up completely. 'Socially inept', Justin calls me."

"Well, I'm glad." Blake shuddered at the thought of another man's hands touching his beautiful Max. "Time to take you home, where you belong."

The short journey was made in silence. Max dozed fitfully in the passenger seat, still a little green around the edges. When they got back to Watersmeet, Blake ushered him inside, dosed him with a couple of Advil then put him to bed. "You need to sleep, Max. We'll start afresh when you're feeling better."

Max nodded drowsily and curled into a ball. Seconds later, he was fast asleep. Blake looked down on him, smiling. *Letting go is easier when you aren't feeling one hundred percent, isn't it, Max?* He doubted that Max would be quite so compliant once he recovered. Still, he was in Blake's bed, exactly where he should be. Blake would have preferred to add some ropes or chains to keep him there but didn't think Max would appreciate waking up in bondage. It was a definite option for the future, though. Blake stood and watched him sleep for a while. Leaving Max alone had driven him to drink. Blake would never allow that to happen again.

He wandered downstairs to his study and switched on the computer. He enjoyed working from home because it

95

gave him more time to think. Maybe it was time to make a few changes and do it more often. With Max safe and close by, Blake felt more at ease than he had in weeks. He shook his head wryly—it was a good job that Max didn't realize just how much power he had over him. He made a quick call to his housekeeper and, after catching up on a few domestic issues, ensured that he would have the house to himself for the next two days.

He checked in with Amanda next. She was much more than a personal assistant and knew as much about the running of Armacom as he did. He let her dictate his priorities for the next few hours then got down to a productive morning's work. For lunch he ate some of Amanda's care package before getting straight back to it, resisting the urge to check up on Max. He wanted to get ahead and free up some time over the next couple of days. He spoke to Amanda several more times, took a couple of conference calls and by six was satisfied with what he had accomplished. He powered down his computer and leaned back in his chair, rolling his shoulders. *Time to lever Max out of bed.*

Blake decided to get some dinner going before he woke Max but when he reached the kitchen he was surprised to find Max already there, puttering around. He watched silently from the doorway, admiring Max's fluid, graceful movements. He was barefoot, dressed in jeans and T-shirt once more, and when he bent to pull something from the fridge the denim hugged his ass perfectly.

"Mm. Very nice." Blake ogled him shamelessly. "Though I'm sure you would be much more comfortable naked, and no, that's not a veiled instruction."

Max turned with a start and blushed to the roots of his hair. "I… I thought I would make us some dinner. I slept all day and then I didn't want to disturb you while you were working…Sir." He added the honorific after a moment's hesitation. He had good instincts.

Blake took a seat at the kitchen table. "That's a lovely idea, thank you. You carry on and let me know if there's anything you'd like me to do." He watched Max's every move, taking great delight in his nervous awareness of being scrutinized. He was pleased that Max had taken the initiative. He would need regular tasks to own, and if he enjoyed cooking, creating meals for them could be part of his new routine.

"So what culinary delight are you conjuring up?"

"Grilled chicken with salsa and wild rice. Will that be okay, Sir? I need to learn about your likes and dislikes."

"Sounds delicious. I'm not fussy when it comes to food, though I don't eat much red meat. You'll soon get to know my tastes...in all things." He grinned. "You know this doesn't let you off punishment, don't you?"

Max leaned against the sink, hiding, not making eye contact. "I guessed you wouldn't forget."

"You guessed right. I have a really good memory when it comes to disobedience, though your confession wasn't *that* long ago. I want you to look at me when I'm talking to you, Max."

Max turned slowly, resisting every inch of the way. Blake could see the tension in his body and the willpower it took Max to meet his eyes.

"You want this. You need it. You deliberately touched yourself without permission last night because you knew I would be obliged to punish you. I have to be consistent with my rules, Max."

"I don't... I'm not sure. I'm scared."

"Scared of me?" Blake felt his stomach clench.

"Scared of the way you make me feel. Last night I felt guilty for touching my own cock, for Christ's sake. You're in my head. That's what you've done to me in a few short days. This... All this can't be real."

"You think it's just a game? Some kind of fantasy?" Blake stood and pulled Max into his arms, wrapping him up tight. "This is the way I live my life and I want you to be part of it. Nerves are natural but I don't ever want you to be afraid."

"I feel like I'm going to wake up and find out it was just

97

a dream, like in one of those God-awful soap opera plot lines."

Blake chuckled and stroked Max's hair. "Don't you want it to be real?"

Max clung to him like a drowning man. "Yes, God help me, I do. But you have to teach me… I don't know what to do, how to be what you want me to be."

"I want you to be yourself, Max, brilliant and beautiful. Don't try to analyze the way you feel—that's the scientist in you, always needing answers. But there is no right and wrong when it comes to submission, just what works for us."

Max gazed up at him, eyes glittering with amusement. "And there was me thinking it was about you always being right and me doing what you tell me?"

"Well, there is that…" Blake let Max go then gave him a sharp smack on the ass. "Finish dinner, then I can make a start on re-educating you."

Max proved to be an excellent cook. They ate in the kitchen rather than the more formal dining room, and the food was delicious, their conversation relaxed. Blake loved that he could talk about subjects dear to his heart with someone intelligent and insightful. When he wasn't worrying about what was going to happen to him next, Max lost his timidity and voiced his opinions with conviction. Intellectually he was Blake's equal and then some.

Eventually they finished their meal. Max cleared away the dishes without being prompted, service coming to him so naturally. By the time he'd washed and dried the last glass, polishing it to a shine, the tension in the air was palpable. Blake took him into the lounge, where an open fire crackled in the grate. He wanted a different venue from the previous evening even though the snug was more intimate. The large room was still warm and cozy despite its size. The two huge leather sofas were scattered with cushions in a range of fabrics—silk, suede and chenille. There was no television, just shelves and shelves of books. Blake switched on the sound system and the room filled with the soft harmonies of classical music. He turned at looked at Max. "I'm glad I went to the trouble of lighting the fire earlier. It's nice and warm in here."

"It's a gorgeous room and I love how many open fires you have."

"They take some work, but I think they're worth it. An open fire is the perfect focal point and I find the flames relaxing to watch." Blake chose not to mention that watching Max clean the fire out naked, ass in the air, would be even more relaxing.

"Watersmeet is beautiful, what I've seen of it so far."

"I've been remiss, I still haven't shown you the grounds, have I? Well, that can wait until tomorrow. I want you to meet my housekeeper at some point as well. If you're going to stay here, Ada will need to get to know you. I can introduce you to the others when the opportunity arises. You've already met Sam, of course."

"Do they…? I mean are they aware…?" Max clamped his mouth shut as if he regretted opening it in the first place.

"Do they know I'm gay?" Blake asked.

"Yes. I mean, I don't know if you're out to everyone. I wouldn't want to say something I shouldn't."

"All my staff here know, not that they would dream of questioning who I choose to bring here as a guest. I want you to feel at home, Max. It's important to me that you're comfortable here."

"It would be hard not to be," Max said. "Physically, that is. Psychologically, I'm not so sure. This world, your world, is all so new to me, and besides, I'm not sure I've forgiven you and Justin yet for talking about me behind my back." His eyes twinkled.

Blake stood with his back to the fire, letting warmth soak into his bones. "Your brother cares about you very much, Max. Don't blame him. I am entirely at fault. I had my eye on you for so long, but you came across as unattainable and I'm afraid I can't resist a challenge. When Justin let slip

99

that you liked me, I moved a little quicker. It would have happened eventually without his prompting."

Max gave a disbelieving grunt.

"You don't believe me?" Blake asked.

"I know my brother. He thinks I need to be taken care of, protected. He forgets I have a mind of my own."

"A very bright mind," Blake stated.

"We're some pair, though, because I was watching you too. I thought you were so far out of my league that a secret crush was all I would ever have."

Blake chuckled. "Then we were clearly destined to be together, don't you think? Take a seat, Max."

Max perched on the edge of a sofa cushion, hands clasped tightly.

"You're highly intelligent. You wouldn't be here if, deep down, you didn't want to be."

Max ducked his head, examining his hands.

"And if that changes, all you have to do is say so. I have very few rules—it keeps things simple, easy for you to remember."

Max nodded nervously.

"Often in a D/s relationship there's a written contract between the couple. I don't propose to introduce one of those unless you specifically require it."

"I don't think that's necessary, Sir. I'd rather we just talked things through."

"That's fine. You may call me Blake, or address me as Sir if it sits easier with you. I may specifically ask you to use Sir or Master in a scene."

"A scene?" Max asked. "I mean, I know what a scene is but you're a lifestyle Dom. You don't switch it on and off."

"True, but sometimes I might want to indulge in some role play or create a specific atmosphere. If that's the case I'll let you know. The second rule is you ask me if there is anything you don't understand. There are no punishments for questions. For me, this is who I am—it's not a game and you need to understand where I'm taking you."

"Yes, Sir."

"I will never mark you permanently or humiliate you. Okay so far?"

Max nodded, eyes wide.

"Good. Now, I want you to choose a new safeword—I don't want Ella Preston in my head when we're together. Ever."

Max giggled, the sound sweet to Blake's ears. "Okay, Sir."

"I didn't ask you before—have you ever used a safeword with anyone else?"

"No, Sir. I haven't... I mean I've always found strong men appealing but I don't have much experience at all. Even at school I was too busy studying for much of a social life. I've messed around, but that's it. How the hell do you explain to a prospective boyfriend that you want him to spank you and tie you up? And I was never brave enough to go to a club that might fulfill those needs for me."

Blake smiled and felt his cock twitch. Max was an untouched canvas that he couldn't wait to add his own colors to. "Well, think of something, other than Preston, that you wouldn't use in everyday conversation. You scream 'no' or 'stop' and nothing will happen. It could just be part of a role you're playing—unwilling slave boy or a captive prince perhaps."

"Oh, that sounds amazing."

"I decide when to stop if you don't use your safeword."

"How about 'Argon'? Will that be okay, Sir?"

"Any particular reason?" Blake was curious.

"Well, it's used for blanketing reactive elements and as a protective atmosphere for growing things like silicon crystals. It feels safe."

"You realize it's also used for welding? Hot and fiery."

Max nodded. "Nice juxtaposition, isn't it?"

Blake shook his head in amusement. "Argon it is. Though I can't believe you managed to turn a safeword into a scientific conversation." He took a seat on one of the sofas and pointed to the rug in front of it.

"Take off your clothes then come and kneel here."

Max stood up but an agony of indecision crossed his face. Blake waited patiently for Max's inner struggle to run its course, then concealed a sigh of pleasure as Max revealed his body, slowly stripping off his T-shirt and jeans. His soft, fitted boxers were tented nicely. He shoved them down and off quickly then knelt with his hands cupped over his crotch.

"Look at me, Max." Blake kept his voice gentle because Max seemed absolutely petrified. "You obeyed, if a little slowly. That's good, but you must never cover yourself in front of me. Please put your hands behind your back."

When Max complied, Blake stood and went across to a bookshelf where a shiny pair of rigid cuffs sat waiting. Max twisted, watching him anxiously, but he didn't bolt when Blake snapped the metal around his wrists. To Blake, he seemed more at ease, an almost imperceptible change in his posture giving him away. His cock certainly didn't object, standing hard and proud away from his body. Blake took hold of a few strands of soft blond hair and tugged Max's head back, not to hurt him but to exert control.

"Do you understand why you are going to be punished?"

"Yes, Sir. You made it very clear. I touched myself and I came when you told me not to. Again."

"You also hid from me, got drunk and made yourself ill. That's not acceptable, Max. If you're worried or scared you talk to me."

"Yes, Sir."

"Very well. You have your safeword. Remember, there's no shame in using it."

Max nodded, pulling against Blake's hold on his hair.

Blake made himself comfortable on the sofa and patted his lap. "Come here, across my lap."

Max made a fair attempt at getting up gracefully with his bound hands. Positioning himself across Blake's lap was more difficult. Blake balanced him with firm pressure on the small of his back, settling him so that Max's cock was snug between Blake's thighs and his pretty ass raised up. He submitted beautifully, not struggling or protesting. Blake stroked the smooth, pale skin lovingly, relishing the thought that it would soon bear his marks.

Max whimpered, and Blake gave him a reassuring pat. "You're completely safe, sweetheart, I won't let you fall. You are stunning and you're doing so well."

"I'm so turned on, but I don't know why, Sir. It doesn't make sense."

"It doesn't have to. Feel, don't think."

Even with the crackle of the fire and the hum of classical music providing background ambience, the sound of his hand making contact with Max's skin seemed unnaturally loud. Blake paused after the single strike, giving Max time to absorb the sensation. Blake hadn't hit him as hard as he could, nor had he been gentle. The heat enveloping Blake's palm would be magnified a thousand times over for Max. Max's skin blushed a light shade of pink. Blake rubbed Max's smooth cheeks, knowing it would dissipate any residual stinging.

"Okay?" Blake felt the need to check. If Max wasn't so unschooled, Blake would have carried on at his own pace.

"More, Sir." Max squirmed on his lap.

"This is a punishment, not a treat, Max." Blake shook his head.

"Yes, Sir. Of course."

"Brat."

Clearly Max didn't need to be pampered. Blake flexed his fingers and began to discipline Max in earnest. He built up a steady rhythm, maintaining the same force, spanking firmly and steadily. He warmed each cheek and the top of Max's thighs, spacing his strokes, never striking in the same place twice. Under his hand, Max's flesh warmed and flushed from pink to a rosy crimson. Max moaned and made the sweetest little noises that got louder and turned into curses as Blake continued.

"Stop! Please... Sir! Oh!"

103

Blake ignored Max's pleas and continued until he judged his fledgling sub had reached the edge of his tolerance. Max hadn't used his safeword but tears were running down his cheeks and he sobbed quietly. Blake reached between Max's spread thighs and grasped his cock. It felt hot and hard in his hand, the tip slick with pre-cum. He stroked him roughly, squeezing the rigid flesh, rubbing his thumb over the head.

"You have my permission to come, Max."

Spurts of creamy warmth filled Blake's hand almost instantly as Max's muscles spasmed and he came with a yell. Then his body sagged bonelessly across Blake's lap. Blake helped him up then settled him on the couch with a cozy throw over him, before going to clean up. He brought water back with him and took the bottle to Max's dry lips. He greedily sucked the cool liquid down before peeking at him through his lashes. Blake detected a sparkle in his eyes that had nothing to do with remorse.

"Am I forgiven, Sir?"

Blake sighed. "I have a feeling I need to come up with a punishment you don't enjoy quite so much." He undid the handcuffs and massaged the reddened skin around Max's slim wrists. "Now, back on your knees while I go and find a nice comfortable cage for your cock."

Max looked horrified. "But, Sir! You can't... I took my punishment."

"This is about control, Max, not punishment." He took hold of Max's dick. "This belongs to me now and if I want to wrap it up safe and sound, then I will. You just wait here and think about how it's going to feel when I fuck you in chastity." He dropped a cushion on the floor and waited for Max to kneel.

Max winced as his ass met his heels.

Blake headed for the door, grinning to himself. Right then he couldn't imagine his world being any more perfect.

# Chapter Nine

Max took a few deep breaths. There wasn't a paper bag in sight so hyperventilating was not an option. He decided that focusing on his surroundings rather than his heated ass might be a wise idea. The room he was in was huge. His whole apartment could probably fit inside it with a bit of space left over. As he gazed around at the expensive, understated furnishings he began to realize just how wealthy Blake was. Of course he was aware that Blake owned Armacom, but Watersmeet was the home of someone who had reached the upper echelons of society.

"He's absolutely loaded. What the hell am I doing here?" Left alone in the lounge, panic built inside him. Blake's presence was an anchor for his sanity and without him Max drifted, lost on a wave of emotion that threatened to overwhelm him. He stared at a painting on the opposite wall. It wasn't huge, but it seemed vaguely familiar. Max wasn't an art connoisseur but he knew enough to recognize a Monet. "Holy fuck." The jewel-like colors blurred and his stomach lurched.

Max spotted his discarded clothes on a chair. Leaving his cushion wasn't advisable but he did it anyway. He grabbed his jeans, pulling them on as quickly as he could. When the fabric brushed his ass he gasped, then moaned. "I'm losing my mind." Lusting after Blake from afar was one thing, but the man had just put him in handcuffs and spanked him. Even worse, Max had loved every minute of it. He'd had the best orgasm in living memory and really, really wanted more of those. He couldn't find his shoes or socks. Then he remembered, he'd left them in the bedroom. Blake's bedroom! *Oh God – that huge, gorgeous bed – comfortable and soft and...* Oh, how he'd dreamed of sharing it with Blake. He couldn't focus – his mind was skittering around all over the place. Shoes... Irrelevant, he'd come in Blake's car, hadn't he? There was no way to get home.

Still shirtless, he was pacing up and down when Blake came back. Max had no idea how long Blake had been observing him from the doorway. He froze, not knowing what to say or do. Then Blake walked toward him and enveloped him in a hug. He shuddered in Blake's hold, repressing a sob but feeling safe and protected. He tried to pull away. "I can't do this, Blake... I just... This was a mistake." He struggled harder but Blake just held him tighter.

"Would you like to tell me what happened to frighten you between me leaving the room and now?"

The rumble of Blake's deep voice vibrated through Max's body.

"If you don't tell me what's going through that brain of yours, Max, I can't help."

Max shook his head and let himself go limp. "I want to go home. Can I call a taxi?"

Blake stroked his hair. "If you really want to leave, I'll drive you home myself." He moved his hold to Max's shoulders then cupped his face. "I don't think that *is* what you want, though, is it?"

Max didn't dare move or speak because Blake was right. He didn't want to go but he had to. Blake was so far out of his league he was in another stratosphere. There was no way that for Blake this could be anything more than a brief diversion. Max accepted that Blake was a genuine Dominant and when he said it wasn't a game to him he was telling the truth, but why would someone like Blake ever choose a shy, clumsy geek like him? Max didn't think he could bear being dumped. Blake was everything he had ever dreamed of but that was what he was, just a dream. He had to be realistic. Better to stop this now before he got

106

hurt, because that was becoming inevitable. Blake stroked his face and he whimpered softly.

"I can't..."

"You can't what, Max? Tell me. How can I help you if you won't tell me what's wrong?"

The appeal in Blake's voice broke through Max's scant defenses and he crumbled into the truth. "The way you make me feel, Blake, you light me up inside. I can't stand the thought of never knowing that again."

"And what on earth makes you think you won't?"

"You could have anyone..." A hot tear rolled down his cheek, and Blake brushed it away with the pad of his thumb.

"Oh, Max. I went to a lot of trouble to get you to myself. I have no intention of ever letting you go."

Max gazed up into a very serious expression. "Never?"

"Never." Blake spoke very firmly. "I didn't want to push you too fast, Max, but I've wanted you for a long time. From the moment you first walked into my world."

"But that was over two years ago!"

"That's right. I think I've been very patient, don't you? I don't want or need anyone else. I want you."

"But you're so...so..." Max stuttered helplessly.

"Rich?" Blake chuckled. "That's true. Sorry, but there's not much I can do about that. But money can't buy me the right person. If it could, I might have offered you a magnificent bribe instead of cooking up that little experiment you couldn't refuse. Think about it—do you really believe Justin would have given me his blessing if he suspected I was just going to use you?"

The burn of shame heated Max's cheeks. "I'm so dumb... I'll go..."

Blake growled, "You're going nowhere. Now remove those annoying pants before I rip them off."

That commanding tone was exactly what Max needed. Blake's reassurances had calmed him and having an order to obey was perfect. He stripped quickly, and when Blake took his hand, followed him to the bedroom without resisting.

"It seems that my slow and steady approach gives you far too much time to worry. That's something I should have anticipated when thinking too much is what I pay you for!"

A gentle push on his shoulder prompted Max to drop to his knees. "Sometimes, it's nice not to have to think."

Blake tugged gently on his hair, pulling his head back. "I'm glad you realize that. When we're playing, you won't have time to analyze everything, just to do as I say."

"And when we're not *playing*, Sir?"

"If we're alone, you are my submissive and will behave as such. If I take you out to a club, the same applies. At work, no one needs to know. I will not hide that we are together, but the nature of our relationship is no one's business but ours."

Max blinked. "I don't know *how* to behave as a submissive, Sir. I've never done this with anyone else."

Blake ruffled his hair. "You're doing fine, Max. Submission comes naturally to you and there is no right or wrong way to behave. I expect you to be obedient, to make your body available to me. In return, I will give you clear instructions, structure and protection. Spread your knees wider."

Max shifted and tried not to think about how exposed he was. "Why protection, Sir? Being your submissive doesn't put me in danger, does it?"

Blake chuckled. "Oh, sweetheart, if I take you out, every Dominant who sees you will want you. You're mine. I don't share."

Max was confused. "I don't understand. I have no experience, why would anyone else want me?"

Blake touched his shoulder lightly. "You really have no idea how beautiful you are, do you? Pretty, innocent, willing to learn—I should put you in chains and never let you out of my sight." He walked over to the dresser and picked up something shiny. "But for now, I'm just going to lock up your dick. Sit on the edge of the bed."

Max swallowed but did as he'd been told. Blake tapped

a knee and he spread himself wide. Blake showed him the device he was holding.

"Have you seen anything like this before?"

"Only on the Internet, Sir. Never in real life."

"Well, I could have chosen something lighter, but I want you to know you're wearing this. You'll feel its weight and think of me. Here, take it and have a look."

Max handled the contraption curiously — it was smoothly polished and heavier than he thought it would be.

"It's fairly obvious how it works, the thick ring fits around the base of your balls, while your shaft goes in here." Blake indicated the steel spirals that formed a tube. "You can shower and use the bathroom with it on."

Max handed the device back to Blake. "Why do you want me to wear it, Sir?" He jerked as Blake handled his dick and balls, sliding the metal rings into their correct positions.

"You won't be able to come while you're wearing this. Denying you release is something I'll enjoy greatly. It will help you understand that your body is mine, to do with as I please. There. Perfect."

Max looked down at his groin and whimpered. His poor cock was encased in rings of metal, the base of his balls gripped snugly by a thick steel band. A small but weighty padlock joined the two sections and there was no sign of a key.

"Oh... I... How long do I have to keep it on, Sir?" Secretly he thought that ten minutes would be more than adequate.

"Until I decide it can come off."

There wasn't anywhere else to go with that statement. Blake began to undress, providing Max with a welcome distraction. His body was stunning — defined and muscular. Max couldn't tear his eyes away — though he'd seen Blake naked, this was the first time that he had long enough to truly examine Blake's cock. It was something he would never forget. Blake was well over six feet tall and quite broad. His cock was perfectly in proportion — thick, hard and powerful like the rest of him. The dark hair at his groin was trimmed to stubble and his balls hung heavy and smooth. Max caught himself licking his lips. He really wanted another taste but didn't know if he was allowed to ask. He wondered if begging might work.

Blake climbed onto the bed and sat with his back against the headboard, one leg bent, the other stretched out. He looked so confident and relaxed. Tentatively, Max crawled up to kneel between his thighs. He gave Blake a pleading look and was rewarded with a nod. *Oh! Perfect.* He reached out to touch, anticipating the velvety smoothness.

"No hands, Max. Put them behind your back."

Blake's smile was just a little bit evil.

Max scowled but did as he'd been told, twining his fingers together. It made balancing difficult as he leaned forward, putting noticeable strain on his thigh and stomach muscles. None of that mattered when he wrapped his lips around the head of Blake's cock and tasted him. Somehow it was different from the first time. Then, he'd been exhausted and overwrought, now he could savor every sensation. Max lapped eagerly at a tiny bead of pre-cum. It was delicious, a little salty but not too bitter. He ran his tongue around the plump head, then down the silky shaft to mouth Blake's balls. He hummed happily. Blake wasn't telling him to stop, so he had to be doing something right. He turned his attention back to Blake's stiff cock. He'd had trouble taking it all the first time—he was determined to do better this time. He adjusted his angle then took the long shaft into his mouth. When the tip touched the back of his throat, he breathed hard through his nose, controlling his gag reflex, then relaxed his throat and bent forward.

"Oh Christ!"

Max smiled inside at Blake's exclamation and swallowed, knowing that the constriction of his throat would compress the head of Blake's dick nicely. Running out of breath, he withdrew, sucked happily then plunged down again. His mouth was so full and Blake tasted delicious. He could do this all night! He felt Blake's fingers tangle in his hair, steadying him. There was no pressure or force but Blake's hold helped him balance and relieved the tension in his muscles. He was vaguely aware of the heat in his own balls and his cock's fruitless struggle to harden in its cage, but his frustration didn't matter. He was focused on Blake and he used every trick he knew with tongue and teeth to give his Master pleasure.

"Close!"

Blake's voice was broken. Max had no intention of pulling away. He wanted to take everything Blake could give him. He drew him in deep again and Blake came hot and hard into his throat. Max swallowed repeatedly, determined not to lose a drop, and when Blake stilled he licked him clean before sitting back on his heels.

Blake patted the bed next to him. Max crawled up then stretched out, pressing close to Blake's side. He wanted to cuddle but wasn't sure if that was allowed — Blake didn't seem like the soppy type. Then he was pulled onto Blake's chest and held tight. It was nice to be wrong.

"That was wonderful, Max, thank you."

Max snuggled into the curve of Blake's neck. "My pleasure, Sir."

He felt so content as Blake pulled the covers over them. Max couldn't imagine anywhere he'd rather be. Blake stroked his back and he wanted to purr like a kitten.

"Are you still scared, Max?"

Blake moved his hand lower, rubbing the top of his ass. Max took a moment and tried to think straight. He was a bit fuzzy. Getting his jumbled thoughts in order was a challenge. "No, not scared, Sir. Is nervous anticipation okay?"

Blake pressed a finger between Max's ass cheeks, exploring. He trembled.

"Anything you feel is fine. I told you, there's no right or wrong here. The only rules are those we agree on between us."

Blake turned him over, apparently to gain better access to

111

his ass. Max clenched his muscles as Blake circled his hole with a fingertip, teasing the sensitive skin. He hooked one leg across Blake's thigh, opening himself wider.

"Sweet boy." Blake teased and played, touching and brushing, nothing more. "Are you a virgin?"

Max hid his face in Blake's chest and nodded. He couldn't concentrate with all the sensations Blake's touch was generating.

"You don't have to be embarrassed. You have no idea how honored I am to be the first man you trust enough to do this with."

Max squirmed and pushed against Blake's finger, craving more.

"Let me get some lube, I don't want to hurt you." Blake rummaged in the bedside table with one hand. Max clung to him, unwilling to let go. Blake's touch left his ass for a moment and when it returned, it was slick and cool.

Max squeezed his eyes shut as Blake applied a little pressure to his hole. He tried to relax, to let him in, but his body fought back. He whimpered.

"Hush now." Blake rubbed his lower back. "Don't think, just feel, remember?"

The pressure against his entrance returned but this time Max gave in. Blake's finger slipped into him.

"Oh! That's… Oh!" There was a tingling burn, but the sensation of something inside his channel was overwhelming. "So good." He wriggled impatiently. "More please, Sir!"

"Demanding brat." Blake chuckled.

Max felt more pressure, then a stretch. Another finger! There were two now, moving, exploring. It was strange but good. Then Blake touched something inside him and the world exploded in a scatter of bright lights. His cock fought to swell but couldn't, his balls drew up tight against his body.

"Feels spectacular, doesn't it?" Blake was rubbing that special spot and Max couldn't think or breathe or see.

"Sir! Please! Oh please… I need to come!" Then his body was empty, aching, frustrated.

"You need to, but you can't. Isn't it perfect?"

Blake was squeezing his balls lightly, torturing him. "Bastard! Stop!"

"Now that's no way to talk to your Master, Max. I believe that's three you've earned." Blake's voice was full of amusement.

"Four, Sir," Max admitted. "I swore when you were out of the room earlier."

"Four it is. I appreciate your honesty. You need to learn patience, discipline. Just think how good it will be when you finally have my cock inside you, stretching you, filling you."

Max sobbed. It was too much. In that moment he hated Blake *and* loved him. He wanted to run away, he wanted to cling on for dear life. Blake leaned across him and pulled something up from beneath the bed. Max didn't realize what was going on until cold metal snapped closed around his wrist.

"Just in case you have any plans to run away."

Before Max could protest, Blake kissed him. He was rough and demanding, plunging his tongue into Max's mouth. Max opened to him. There was no other choice. He felt as if his bones were melting. No one had ever kissed him with such possessive passion before. When Blake rolled away, Max gasped for air, shivering with pleasure.

"Sleep now. It's late." Blake pulled him close.

Max listened to Blake's breathing as it slowed. How could the man just switch off like that? It wasn't fair. Max was painfully aware of his caged cock, of the chain attached to his wrist. He was never going to be able to sleep. His body, physically and emotionally shattered, decided otherwise and seconds later he slipped into welcoming darkness.

# Chapter Ten

The next morning, Blake woke earlier than usual. The sun had barely risen and the dawn chorus was in full swing. He fought back a smile as Max appeared from the en-suite bathroom and glanced nervously at the bed. Blake had released him to freshen up but only on the condition that he came straight back to be chained again. He was so tempting with his hair mussed from sleep — his big blue eyes, wide, giving him an air of bemused wonder. The cage around his cock gleamed — it suited him and Blake was glad that he had chosen it over the acrylic alternatives. He owned a selection, and there would be plenty of opportunity to put the others to good use.

Max gave a pensive little sigh. He cocked his head to one side.

"Is this really necessary?" He climbed back into bed.

"It is." He smelt of soap and toothpaste. Blake needed to wash too but didn't want to risk Max bolting while he wasn't around to stop him. Despite Blake's reassurances, Max was still skittish, something that was entirely understandable. Blake might come across as paranoid but he didn't care. Max wouldn't run before Blake had the opportunity to talk him down. He locked the cuff around Max's wrist again, checking that there was plenty of slack in the chain fixed to the bed frame. It was lightly padded and even overnight it had only left a slight mark on Max's skin. Blake was content that there was no pressure on an artery — Max's circulation would be fine.

"I won't be long." He climbed out of bed, adjusted the comforter to cover Max's bare chest, then headed for the

114

shower. He stood beneath the powerful spray and closed his eyes, trying to get his scattered thoughts in order. Max had a way of diverting him from a carefully planned course of action with nothing more than a flutter of his lashes. Blake was unaccustomed to feeling nervous but his guts were twisted into knots that morning. He'd told Max their experiment was over, but it was Friday and they had an understanding. If Max insisted on leaving that evening, Blake would have no choice but to let him go, and that was the last thing he wanted. He was already pushing boundaries by flouting his own rules. Three hours a night for five nights, that was the deal, so why was this beautiful young man chained to his bed first thing in the morning? He wasn't usually so undisciplined.

Blake soaped and shampooed beneath the reviving spray. Deep down, he knew why he had willingly changed his plans but it was hard for him to admit.

"Shit, I've fallen in love with him." Realization swamped him. Max Allenby had stolen his heart. He rested his head on the cool tiles. He'd tried to resist but from the moment Max had walked into Armacom, he'd been smitten. Something about Max had called to him from the start. He'd tried to stay detached, deliberately avoiding the labs, but Justin Allenby had noticed the surreptitious glances sent his brother's way.

At first Blake had denied any interest but it wasn't in him to be dishonest. He'd faced up to Justin but assured him that he wouldn't act on his attraction. It wasn't appropriate. Blake turned off the shower and grabbed a towel from the heated rail. Fortunately his head of security had disagreed. Justin was a protective older sibling and saw Blake as the perfect prospective brother-in-law. Now Blake hoped he would be able to live up to the expectation.

It was Justin who had given Blake insider information about Max, letting him know that he hardly ever dated and had a personal rule about avoiding getting involved with work colleagues. Blake gave himself a brisk rub down, enjoying the memory of how he had persuaded Justin to part with titbits of information about his younger brother. It had been several long, frustrating months before the right opportunity to employ his knowledge had come along. When Max had abruptly introduced himself to Blake's car bumper, he'd opened a door that Blake was only too eager to go through.

He finished drying and wrapped the towel round his hips while he brushed his teeth. He wiped a streak across the misted mirror and gave his reflection a critical look. Was he being too manipulative? Max had to make his own choices without feeling compelled. Blake wanted a submissive, a lover, he didn't want a slave. Part of Max's attraction was his mind — Blake had to make sure Max knew that submission didn't mean he had to change. He just had to be himself.

Blake hung his towel on the rail. He debated shaving but decided that stubble would make interesting patterns on Max's skin, so he left it. His beard grew in quickly but it could wait until the evening. He threw on his robe and returned to the bedroom. Max was sitting against the pillows looking ridiculously pretty but a little annoyed.

"I think you need coffee, sweetheart," Blake suggested. "Stay put while I go and make some." He tightened the belt around his robe.

Max tugged on his chain. "I'm hardly going anywhere, am I?"

"True." Blake ignored the petulance. "It's where I want you, so there you'll stay." He went downstairs to find caffeine. They could both do with a shot or two and there would be plenty of time to address Max's attitude later. That thought gave him a warm fuzzy feeling. "Losing it. I'm definitely losing it." It made a pleasant change from his usual rigid self-control. Max was making gradual but inexorable inroads into his defenses.

When he reached the kitchen, Blake could see that Ada had already been in that morning. She preferred to get an early start and was probably already on her way to

116

the market. Everything was spotless and there were fresh flowers in a vase on the windowsill. Blake sent her a short text to explain that he would be working at home again that day. They had their own signaling system. If the door to a room was closed, Ada didn't go through it. It ensured Blake had privacy when he needed it and meant that Ada could get on with her work in other parts of the house. When Blake returned to the bedroom with two mugs of freshly brewed coffee and a plate of hot buttered toast on a tray, he made sure to close the door very firmly behind him. Ada would be back at some point to stock the fridge and complete her cleaning duties.

Max was fiddling with the cuff around his wrist, frowning thoughtfully. Blake put his coffee on the bedside table. He handed Max the other mug, then settled the plate of toast where they could both reach it. The empty tray, he slid under the bed where there was no danger he would step on it. Keeping his robe on, he climbed into bed. He enjoyed knowing that beneath the covers Max was naked and deliciously vulnerable. He sipped his drink and waited for the inevitable questions.

"Why the chain, Blake? Don't you trust me?" Max made the metal jingle.

Blake broke off a piece of toast and held it to Max's lips. To his delight, Max didn't hesitate and took it from his fingers.

"It's got nothing to do with trust, though I really don't want you running away from me. Keeping you in bondage gives me pleasure, it's as simple as that. Be honest, Max, how does it make you feel knowing that you are at my mercy?"

He fed Max another piece of toast and watched as he nibbled it, then licked a stray crumb from his lip. He managed to make even that small act sensual, and Blake's cock plumped in appreciation.

"I... I like it. A lot. But I don't understand why."

"But you're annoyed that I've restrained you?"

"No, that's not it. I'm not being fair. I'm annoyed at

117

myself because you putting me in chains turns me on." Max ducked his head, suddenly shy again.

Blake gently tilted Max's chin up and kissed him. "Mm. You're all buttery." He ran his tongue along Max's lower lip. "Give it time, Max. You have your safeword. You're bound to be a little confused about your feelings, but know that you can stop this at any time. You are in control."

"Try telling my dick that. It's completely *out* of control, and if it wasn't for this fucking cage..." Max nibbled on a nail until Blake pulled his hand away from his mouth.

"That's five. It's not my habit to converse with genitalia, Max, and anyway I fully approve of the reaction. It's such a shame you're not able to get hard." He whipped back the covers, almost tipping over the toast plate but catching it just in time. He put it safely to one side and drank in the sight of Max's imprisoned cock.

Max started to pull his knees up. Blake shoved them back down. "I've told you before about trying to hide from me. Do I need to spank you again?"

Max's pale cheeks turned a beautiful shade of pink. "No! No, Sir."

"Hmm. I think a daily smack or two across that pretty ass would do you the world of good. However, I have a different plan for keeping you entertained today." Blake slipped his hand into the bedside cabinet drawer and pulled out the bulbous plug he had hidden there. He held it up where Max could see it and stroked the smooth black rubber.

Max's eyes widened. "What exactly do you intend to do with that... Sir?"

Blake couldn't help but smirk. "You're an intelligent man, Max, what do you think I'm going to do with it?"

Max shuffled sideways a little, putting some distance between them. Blake chuckled, "You've had my fingers inside you already, this will help stretch you a little more. I want you ready for me." He grabbed the lube and began to coat the plug.

"But... But it's huge!" Max protested. "That thing is *not* going in me."

"Well, I don't like to boast, Max, but it's nowhere near as big as me. I have several of these in larger sizes. I'm starting you off nice and gently with a relatively modest one." Blake patted Max's thigh. "Hands and knees. Now."

Max gave him a pained look, and for a moment Blake thought he might refuse. He was nervous, and Blake understood completely—everything they were doing was a huge leap of faith for Max. Blake was very proud of how well he was doing. There was an enticing clink of metal as Max swiveled himself into position and got comfortable. Blake knelt behind him, plug in hand, and admired the beautiful sight before him.

*I am a very lucky man.* "Part your legs wider."

Max moved his knees farther apart and Blake grinned as his sweet little rosebud entrance was revealed. He couldn't resist giving Max's smooth cheeks a stroke. Max trembled deliciously and let out a little gasp. Blake slicked a little lube around his hole then blew on the glistening skin. That got him more than a gasp—Max yelped and twisted his head back to glare at him.

"Please, Blake, I'm nervous enough about this without you driving me mad with frustration."

Blake chuckled but relented. He pressed the plug gently but persistently against Max's entrance. Max was tense, but relaxed at the mild pressure. The plug slipped into him easily, much to Blake's satisfaction. He made sure it was fully seated and gave Max's ass a little tap. "Lie on your stomach, sweetheart. Get used to how it feels."

Max collapsed onto his stomach. "Get used to it! Really? You have to be kidding me!"

Blake held back a laugh—Max was delightfully bratty at times. He smacked him firmly, eliciting an indignant yelp.

"I need to get on and start some work. Much as I would love to spend the day in bed tormenting you, I do have a company to run." Blake slipped off the bed regretfully then started to dress. Max rolled onto his back and tugged on the chain around his wrist.

"Please tell me you're not leaving me here like this? Shouldn't I be going to work too?"

Blake buttoned his shirt then fastened his faded black jeans. "I've signed you off for the day, and lucky for you, I do have a bit of sway at Armacom." He sat on the edge of the bed to pull on his socks. "In a moment I'm going to release you. But first, I'm going to replace your cage with a nice tight strap."

He opened the dresser drawer and rummaged around. He'd been collecting all kinds of toys with Max in mind, and it was wonderful to finally get to use some of them. He found what he was looking for and fingered the soft black leather—it was going to contrast perfectly with Max's pale skin.

Blake went to the side of the bed, took a tiny key from his pocket and unlocked the cage that held Max's cock. He removed it very carefully then checked for any soreness. Beneath his gentle touch, Max immediately began to harden.

"I love how responsive you are. So eager for my touch." Blake buckled the strap tightly around the base of Max's dick and stood back to admire his handiwork. "It's not impossible to come while you're wearing this, but it will help you resist. You don't have my permission. Today is about discipline and self-control. It's your chance to spend some time thinking about what you really want, Max."

"Jesus, Blake! Self-control wouldn't be a problem if you stopped touching me!"

"Oh, but I enjoy touching you." Blake circled Max's shaft with his fingers and squeezed lightly. He ran his thumb over the plump head, probing the slit. "Mm. So warm." He laughed as Max bucked into his hand, then let him go.

Max was panting, his eyes screwed shut, muttering curses under his breath. He didn't seem to notice when Blake undid the shackle around his wrist. It would be so easy to give in

120

and let him come. Blake was sorely tempted to forget work, climb back into bed and fuck Max senseless, but he didn't. If the day was to be about discipline and control, then that applied to him just as much as it did to Max. If Max only knew what torment Blake would be suffering when he could look and touch, but not take him fully.

Blake went back to his toy drawer and pulled out a set of matching wrist and ankle cuffs. Fashioned from stiff leather, they felt heavy in his hands. He placed them on the end of the bed.

"Put these on, Max, then when you're ready, come downstairs to my study. You remember where it is?"

Max blinked at him. "Yes, but... You want me to put them on myself?"

Blake nodded. "And make sure the buckles are nice and tight, I don't want the leather chafing your skin."

"What else do you want me to wear?" Max glanced around the room, but his clothes were nowhere to be seen.

"The cuffs and the cock strap are all you'll be wearing today." Blake waited for the explosion.

"No! You can't make me do that!" Max pulled his knees up and hugged them. "You can't..." He looked like he might cry.

"I can and you will because it's what I require." Blake kept his voice calm. "Take your time. My housekeeper has already been and gone. There's no danger of you running into anyone on the way, we are the only people in the house."

Blake turned away. He left the room, pulling the door closed behind him. As he made his way to the study he wondered how long it would take Max to pluck up the courage to do as he'd been told. Less than half an hour was acceptable. Any more than that and he would have to be punished. Blake checked his watch and licked his lips. The anticipation was delicious.

Exactly twenty-nine minutes later there was a soft knock on his study door. Blake pushed his chair back from the desk a little. He wasn't sure whether to be pleased that Max had met his target, or disappointed that the opportunity to administer another punishment had been taken away from him.

"Come in, Max."

The door opened slowly, and Max slid around it. Blake's cock hardened like it was going for some kind of record. Max looked stunning. The black leather at his wrists and ankles set off his pale skin, and the matching strap around the base of his cock and balls pushed them forward provocatively.

"Stand in front of the desk with your legs apart and hands behind your back."

Max complied but kept his eyes downcast. A full body tremble told Blake that Max might bolt at any moment. Blake got up. He crossed the room then locked the door. He circled Max slowly, stroking him with gentle but possessive touches. He wanted Max to get the message that his body now belonged to Blake—every perfect inch of it.

"You look beautiful. You don't need to be shy." Max must be feeling vulnerable, scared and unsure, but his cock was rock hard. There was no doubt that some part of him loved the scene they were playing out. Blake positioned a chair in front of his desk. It had a wide, cushioned seat, splayed legs and an ornately carved back—perfect for displaying his prize.

He guided Max to the chair and sat him down, chuckling at the whimper Max made when his ass hit the seat.

"Enjoying the plug, sweetheart? It makes you aware of every movement, doesn't it?" Blake took a set of leather ties from his desk and used them to attach Max's ankle cuffs to the legs of the chair, forcing him to keep his knees wide apart. He drew Max's arms behind the chair back then tied them loosely together.

"There, now all you have to do is sit quietly and think about how this makes you feel. No speaking unless you want to use your safeword."

Blake returned to his chair, put on his glasses and focused

on his work. There was a sharp intake of breath in front of him, and he looked up to see a new flush on Max's face. Blake suspected it was the glasses—his sweet, innocent Max apparently had a thing for men in specs.

"I'll have to forgo the contact lenses more often." Blake tested his theory. Max's smile was coy, but Blake had guessed correctly.

He wasn't overly productive in the hour that followed. Having the man of his erotic dreams naked and bound right in front of him was somewhat distracting. Max's erection never wavered, his smooth cock curved upward toward his flat belly above balls made plump by the strap beneath them. To begin with, when Blake glanced up from his work, Max would be staring right back at him, flushed and nervous, moments away from panic. As time went on, his gaze dropped and the tension disappeared from his body. His breathing became steadier. When Blake finally decided that it was time for lunch and slid his chair back, Max didn't stir.

Blake smiled—Max seemed content if a bit spaced out, all the worry lines gone from his face. He approached quietly, not wanting to startle him. He stroked Max's hair, marveling at how soft it was and how pretty with the light making it glint like gold.

"You're safe, Max, I'm here. You've done so well, I'm very proud of you." He murmured words of comfort and reassurance as he released Max from the chair, leaving the leather cuffs in place.

"I think I should go home now," Max whispered.

That wasn't what Blake had been expecting Max to say. A knot formed in his gut.

Max raised his head and stared at him with his big blue eyes. "I'm sorry."

"You're not a prisoner, Max, you can leave any time you want to. But can you tell me why first?" Blake fought to stop his hands shaking. This wasn't Max speaking out of panic or fear—his voice was steady and certain.

"I… I think I love you." Max examined the carpet as if it were the most fascinating floor covering ever created.

A warm glow began to spread through Blake's body. He still felt shivery, but not because he was afraid.

"You have to stop trying to run from me, Max. Why would that make you want to leave?"

"Because that's not what you want, is it? You want a submissive who's obedient and willing. You don't want a lover, a…a boyfriend?"

"Drawing conclusions without in-depth research is a bad habit for a scientist." Blake pulled Max into his arms and held him close. "And I dispute your analysis. I think I fell in love with you the first time I saw you." Saying it made it real.

Max snuffled damply against his neck. "Really?"

"Really." Blake stroked Max's back and the swell of his ass. "I think that qualifies you as my boyfriend, don't you?"

"But…you haven't, we haven't… I'm still a— I thought you didn't want me!" His anguished cry pierced Blake's heart.

"Oh, love, you have no idea how much you've tested my willpower. Of course I want you! I want your submission, I want your body… I want to deserve your love."

Max pushed hard against him. "Show me, Blake, please. I want you inside me. I want you to fuck me until I scream."

Blake jiggled the end of the plug seated in Max's ass and kissed away his yelp. "Well then, unless you want me to take you across my desk, we should probably go upstairs. We can save the desk for another occasion, it has interesting possibilities." He walked across to the door and held out a hand. When Max came to him and took it, Blake's contentment was complete.

"Are you going to let me come, Sir?" Max followed him eagerly toward the stairs.

"That depends…"

"On what, Sir?"

"Oh, Max, if I told you, that would be far too easy,

wouldn't it?"

"You're very cruel, Sir." Max didn't sound at all unhappy about that and Blake's answering grin was feral.

"Yes, love. I am."

# Chapter Eleven

Max took some comfort from the strength of Blake's grip on his hand. Blake would keep him safe no matter what — he knew that deep in his bones. It felt wonderful that someone cared so profoundly about him — that it was Blake Winters who felt that way was the chocolate buttercream icing on top of a very large, gooey cake. Max was also terrified. 'Run for the hills screaming like a little girl' terrified. Losing his virginity to a Dom might have featured in his dreams, but he'd never imagined it might become reality.

Questions poured through his mind as he got closer to Blake's bedroom and the point of no return. *Will it hurt? Will I be any good at it? Will Blake be rough or gentle? Will it hurt? Oops — same question again.* He'd spent far too much time surfing the web, exercising an already vivid imagination, in the hope that when the big moment came he would feel prepared. However, that was before Blake had introduced him to a whole new world, a world where soft and gentle didn't seem to exist. No amount of research could make his current situation less daunting.

The fear and uncertainty were kept at bay by the excitement fizzing through his veins. It was as if he'd had an intravenous infusion of champagne and it was making him lightheaded and floaty. He'd felt that way before, sitting in front of Blake's desk, watching him work. At first he'd been mortified — what the hell kind of person sat naked and bound in front of a man like Blake Winters and didn't feel that way? He had a plug up his ass, for Christ's sake.

But as time had gone on, and his erection hadn't diminished, Max had realized that he loved the clarity of

126

absolute submission. His panic had gradually subsided into a feeling of such wonderful peace. He didn't have to worry about anything. He had no decisions to make. He couldn't even move. It was liberating to give himself up that way. His cock liked it too, apparently – of course Blake wearing those sexy specs had helped with that. Max really hoped Blake kept them on in bed.

It was the middle of a bright, sunny day, but when Blake drew the heavy drapes in his bedroom the light dimmed and it could have been any time of day or night. He turned on the small lamps on either side of the bed and fluffed the pillows. Max loved that bed. The thread count on the sheets had to be in the high hundreds they were so soft and smooth, and the duvet was filled with some kind of down. It weighed nothing but was snugly warm and the pillows – Max was very tempted to steal a couple for his own bed. It wasn't flashy or brash, but everything about Blake's bedroom spoke of wealth that Max could hardly imagine.

Only a few short hours earlier, he had sat on the bed trying to pluck up the courage to buckle leather cuffs around his own limbs and walk down the stairs naked, his cock jutting lewdly from a leather ring. He'd put the ankle bands on first, tightening the buckles carefully. He hadn't been able to decide how he felt so he'd put the other pair onto his wrists. They weren't too heavy but he wasn't going to be able to forget they were there. He'd played with the little metal D-rings attached to them and wondered what they might be used for. The more he'd imagined, the harder his cock had become. In the end, he had stopped thinking and moved. It was the only way he was going to make it to Blake's study. The journey down the stairs had only become feasible when he'd kept his mind blank and didn't think about what he was doing.

Now he was back in the bedroom, still naked while Blake remained fully dressed. Max desperately wanted to cover his groin with his hands, but that was likely to earn him a punishment, and the thought of being spanked with the

127

plug inside him made his mouth go dry. He stood still, hands loosely grasped behind his back, legs apart, and waited for Blake to tell him what to do.

Blake finished arranging the bed and beckoned him over. Max's face heated as Blake examined him. He ducked his head a little. Maybe he didn't pass muster. Even after all Blake's reassurances, there was a part of Max that couldn't quite believe a man like Blake could love him. Blake reached out and touched him, running his hand down Max's arm.

"You are utterly beautiful."

Max instantly went all warm and melty inside. At that moment he would do anything that Blake asked, without question. If Blake wanted to take his virginity while he was chained and hanging upside down from the ceiling—that would be just fine. Though he would prefer to be horizontal and comfortable for such a momentous event in his life.

Blake toed off his socks, then with slow, deliberate movements, he unbuttoned his shirt and shucked it off. Max clamped his mouth shut to prevent it gaping, then Blake cupped a hand around the nape of his neck and pulled him forward into a searing kiss. Max sagged against him, knees buckling. Stubble scraped his skin, making his face tingle. An arm around his waist held him tight and safe. He opened to Blake's exploration.

At first, Max remained passive, letting Blake taste him, but soon he couldn't resist a little investigation of his own. He flicked his tongue into the moist heat of Blake's mouth, nervous to start with but then growing in confidence when he wasn't rejected. Blake tasted of sweet mint and bitter coffee. His lips were firm and unyielding. Blake deepened the kiss until Max thought he would run out of breath. When Blake finally pulled away, Max nuzzled happily into the crook of his neck.

Blake stroked his back and the curve of his ass. His hands were warm and smooth, his movements possessive and confident.

"I think this is one of my favorite parts of you," he

murmured, squeezing Max's butt cheeks.

Max wanted to grind against him but instead sank to his knees and looked up in appeal. Blake nodded slightly and wrapped his hand in Max's hair, holding him tight. The tug against his scalp sent a thrill straight to Max's aching dick. Since being with Blake he'd discovered that he loved having his hair pulled.

His fingers were clumsy and uncoordinated. He fought Blake's fly until eventually the annoying zipper slid down. Max mouthed the bulge in the black cotton beneath, pushing and probing with his tongue. A sharp pull on his hair gave him the clear signal he wanted. He slipped his fingers beneath the waistband of Blake's shorts and carefully pulled them down, revealing inch by perfect inch the length of his cock. He kept going until Blake's shorts and trousers were around his ankles and he could kick them off over his bare feet.

Max loved Blake's body. He was lean and toned, his muscles nicely defined. His cock was a work of art, standing thick and proud from his body, his balls smooth and tight. He luxuriated in the heat of Blake's skin. Max sighed happily and flicked his tongue for a taste. The little jewel of pre-cum he lapped up tasted like Blake's mouth, bittersweet. Max murmured happy little sounds and sucked the head of Blake's cock gently. Blake hadn't stopped him from using his hands and he took full advantage, cupping Blake's balls and stroking them in time with his sucking action. He compressed his lips a little and took more of Blake's length into his mouth. Max hollowed his cheeks and sucked hard, bobbing his head quickly. Blake gasped — the first sound he had made — and jerked. Max grabbed Blake's hips, pulling him forward, encouraging him to thrust again.

"Max, love…" Blake pulled his hair hard until he backed off.

Max raised his eyes in confusion, wondering what he had done wrong. It was okay — Blake was smiling. "I want to come inside you, and if you don't stop that's never going to happen." He pulled Max to his feet and wrapped him in a tight embrace. "You have an amazing mouth. You'll get plenty of chances to use it, I promise."

Max tilted his head back and gazed into Blake's eyes. What he saw there thrilled him—love, desire and fierce need. He had created those emotions and that made him feel so strong. All Max's fears faded away. He finally realized that though he craved Blake's dominance, the balance of emotional power between them was equal.

He arched his back and thrust his hips wantonly forward, grinding hard against Blake's cock. Blake chuckled as if he too had detected a subtle change in the dynamic between them.

"So eager. So needy. I think I'd like to hear you beg."

Max gasped as Blake cupped his ass and squeezed hard before parting his cheeks and jiggling the end of the plug. His muscles clenched and his breath quickened as Blake sucked hard on his neck, no doubt marking him. There was too much sensation and Max clung to Blake, squirming helplessly in his arms.

"Please, Sir! Fuck me, please, I need you." Giving Blake his wish was not a problem.

Wordlessly, Blake pushed him back onto the bed, positioning himself between Max's legs.

"I'm not going to fuck you, Max, I'm going to make love to you. I want you to remember this moment for the rest of your life and I don't want your memories ruined by pain. I don't want to hurt you."

"Maybe I want it to hurt." Max quivered as Blake loomed over him.

Blake looked at him speculatively. "Maybe you do. But there's time enough for pain, my love. When you said I was cruel, you weren't wrong. I'll give you all the pain you desire, but not today. Today is special, for me as well as you. It's my job to take care of you."

Max smiled up at him. "I trust you, Blake. You make me feel so safe."

Blake went to remove his glasses but stopped. "You like these, don't you?"

"There's just something about them... They make you look all stern and forbidding."

"And that turns you on, doesn't it, sweetheart?"

Max nodded—there was no point in denying it. "Everything about you turns me on, Sir." He wriggled impatiently. His cock hurt, straining and hard, the strap denying him pleasure. "Please, Blake, please... I ache, I need you!"

"You have me. I'm right here." Blake leaned over him and gave him a deep, lingering kiss.

When Blake slipped his hand between Max's legs, Max sucked in his breath. Blake pulled on the end of the plug. He was slow and careful but Max still gasped until Blake kissed him into breathless silence. With the plug gone, he ached at the emptiness. Blake pressed a finger against his lips. "Hush. Trust me."

Blake reached for the bedside table and grabbed a tube of lubricant. Max watched with nervous excitement as Blake slicked his fingers until they gleamed. Then he rubbed Max's entrance, not penetrating, just moving in slow circles that warmed his skin and made him part his legs wider. He wanted more. Needed it like he needed air.

"Oh! Oh, Blake, Sir! Please!" His vision blurred as Blake breached his channel with a finger and pushed inside him.

There was a tingle of heat as Blake stroked his inner walls, stretching him the slightest amount. Max wanted to scream. He pushed against Blake's touch, trying to drive him in deeper, but Blake was not to be hurried.

"Tell me how it feels..." Blake whispered.

"Too slow! Not enough! Please..." Max bucked and wriggled.

"Careful, brat, or I'll tie you down."

"Oh no! Please don't, Sir, I want to touch you!" Max felt the pounding beat of his heart and the pulse that throbbed in time through his cock.

131

"Then be good."

Max drew in a sharp breath, and held it. Blake must have added a second finger. He could feel the burn now, though it wasn't unpleasant. He remembered that he needed oxygen and went from one extreme to the other, panting hard. "It feels incredible," he whispered, almost to himself. He let his head fall back on to the pillow and closed his eyes, giving up any idea of convincing Blake to move faster. Blake controlled his pleasure and he would move at his own pace.

"Just tell me if I hurt you."

Max moaned and whimpered as he writhed beneath Blake's clever touch. It was as if Blake knew exactly how to twist his fingers to cause the most frustration. When Blake finally withdrew, Max moaned his disappointment, but when Blake's teeth captured an aching nipple and bit down, the sweetness of the pain took his mind off what he'd lost. Blake licked and scraped at the tender nub with his teeth while he pinched and rolled its twin with lube-slicked fingers.

If it weren't for the strap around his cock, Max knew he would have come long ago. When Blake moved away from him, he felt bereft, but the absence didn't last long.

"It's clear you need a little pain with your pleasure." Blake showed him a slender chain, either end capped by a rubber-tipped clamp. Blake flicked his nipple then attached first one clamp, then the other.

"Oh! It hurts!" Max wriggled as the clamps pinched his nipples cruelly, though the initial pain soon faded to a pleasant throbbing ache.

Blake smirked. "There, that's better. Put this on me." He handed Max a shiny foil packet. Max took it, hands shaking.

"We don't need... I mean I've never... And I'm sure you..."

"Sweetheart, I'll get a new blood test as soon as humanly possible but until then I glove up. That's not open for debate."

132

"Yes, Sir." Max ripped open the packet. He rolled the condom slowly over the head of Blake's cock and down his shaft.

Blake handed Max the lube.

"It's like Christmas morning with the best present ever." Max slicked Blake's straining cock with the gel. He took full advantage of his chance to touch, and giggled as Blake's shaft twitched and jerked in his hands.

"You keep doing that and we're going to have to start all over again in a couple of hours!" Blake gasped the words as he held Max's wrists together, keeping him still for a few moments.

"Make love to me, Blake, please." Max couldn't wait any longer.

Blake hooked his arms beneath Max's knees and bent him back. He positioned his cock, pressing the blunt head against Max's opening.

"Try to relax, sweetheart," Blake whispered softly.

Then there were no more words. Max chewed on his lower lip as the head of Blake's cock slipped through his resistant barrier muscle. He panted. The stretch was so much bigger than the plug or Blake's fingers had been and it burned. Blake didn't move and as Max got accustomed to the invader in his body he craved more.

"Please!" He hoped Blake would understand the meaning behind that single word.

Blake pushed and Max's channel stretched to accommodate his cock. There was no stopping now. Blake was in him, filling him. The pain was there but bearable, then Blake brushed his prostate and everything went away. Max thought he screamed, he wasn't sure. Everything was misty and confusing. Then Blake released the leather cock strap and began to move.

"Oh God!" Max wrapped his legs around Blake and pulled him closer, arching beneath him. "Please, please... move!"

Blake grinned down at him. "Demanding brat." But he

133

obliged, beginning slowly, too slowly, drawing out at a snail's pace before he slid forward again. Max thought he would go mad with frustration.

"Harder, damn it, Blake, I won't break!"

Still Blake resisted his pleading, and Max pulled at the bedclothes frantically. "Rough! I want it rough!"

Blake loomed over him, bending him in half. He grabbed his wrists again and held them above Max's head with one hand. Blake drew out again slowly, then he slammed home hard. Max cried out, the pleasure was blinding as Blake thrust again and again. Max begged for more, he couldn't help himself. Blake was holding him down. His nipples burned as the chain between the clamps moved with his writhing body. It was amazing. Perfect.

Max let himself be swallowed by sensation—his orgasm built rapidly and there was nothing he could do to stop it. Blake wasn't even touching his cock, but the hard fast thrusts he was employing were hitting Max's sensitive bundle of nerves every time. Then he came, hard and fast. Heat splashed his belly and chest as his body spasmed again and again. There was one more final penetration then Blake's expression froze in a rictus of pleasure. His hips jerked once and heat filled Max's channel.

"Mine!" Blake shouted as he came.

Max was in no doubt that he had been taken and claimed. As Blake slipped from his body and collapsed next to him on the bed, Max snuggled into him, oblivious to how sticky they both were. He felt safe and loved as Blake pulled him close then yelped as the nipple clamps were removed. "Fuck! That hurts!" He squirmed and whimpered as Blake rubbed the pain away then kissed him hard and deep.

"Mine."

The repetition was hardly necessary. Max knew exactly whom he belonged to, but it still made him feel warm inside.

"Yours, Sir." Whispering the words made him feel complete.

# Chapter Twelve

"Are there any fish?" Max asked, peering into the rushing waters in front of him.

"Plenty." Blake pulled him closer, an arm around his waist. "This is a tiny tributary of the Pemigewasset. I've seen trout and Atlantic salmon jumping here. It's an amazing sight, watching them struggle against the current to get upstream. When it's not quite so turbulent, you can sometimes spot them basking in the shallows as well."

"It's pretty rough at the moment." Max didn't get too close to the edge. The water foamed and frothed as it danced over glistening rocks on the riverbed.

"There's been lots of rain upstream. About a quarter of a mile from here two streams join. The confluence increases the water flow considerably."

"Hence Watersmeet."

"Yes. It seemed appropriate." Blake kissed him, long and slow.

Max leaned into him, inviting him deeper. Blake's kisses were addictive, and Max was firmly hooked. When Blake finally let him go, he gasped for breath.

"Wow!"

Blake chuckled. "I'm flattered by your reaction." He took Max's hand and led him to the picnic rug laid out by the stream. "I don't know about you, but kissing makes me hungry and Ada's picnics are legendary. How about you explore the basket while I pour some drinks?"

Max flopped down on the rug. It was midday and the sun was warm on his face. Contentment permeated every cell of his body. He watched Blake lower himself to the ground. Worn denim hugged his thighs and there was an enticing glimpse of skin where his pale blue cotton shirt was unbuttoned at the neck. His sleeves were rolled up, his strong forearms tanned to gold.

"I wish I went brown in the sun. I just turn bright pink," Max said. He was hungry but in no hurry to eat when he had the gift of time to ogle Blake.

"The joys of such a pale complexion. Still, slathering you in sunscreen was enjoyable." Blake unscrewed the cap on a bottle of fresh orange juice after giving it a quick shake.

Max giggled. The application of lotion had turned into a slippery but exhilarating wrestling match on the bedroom floor, which had culminated in him pinned to the carpet, legs in the air, calves resting on Blake's shoulders. Blake had jacked him off while fucking him with a ridged dildo. Max had come so hard he'd blacked out. When he'd come round, Blake had blindfolded him and fucked his mouth. He fancied that he could still taste Blake's cum.

"May as well take advantage. I don't get to sunbathe very often." Max made sure Blake was watching then whipped off his T-shirt.

Blake's pupils dilated. He ran his tongue across his lower lip, then moved the picnic basket and drinks to a shady spot.

"I think you should finish what you started, don't you? Take off the rest of your clothes."

Max scanned their surroundings anxiously. "What if someone comes?"

"Oh, someone will definitely be coming but it won't be you if you don't do as you're told."

Max's squeak was undignified but warranted in his opinion. They were out of sight of the house and in the private grounds of Watersmeet, but there was still a chance someone on the staff might wander by. He stood, kicked off his sandals, then shimmied out of his jeans. He'd put on the skimpiest underwear from his shopping trip with Cas, thinking he'd be keeping his pants on. Now the white net shorts were a choice he regretted.

"You should go shopping with your friend Cas more often. He has excellent taste."

Sitting on the rug, Max rolled his eyes. "He wanted me to buy leather and latex. These are tame by Cas' standards."

"And you don't like the idea of leather against your skin?"

Not sure how to answer, Max played with the fringed edge of the rug.

"Perhaps you and I should make some choices together. There's an excellent online store I use which has a great range. You certainly have the body for leather."

Heat bloomed in Max's cheeks. His cock hardened.

Blake knelt across him and pushed him down onto the rug. "You started this." He rubbed Max's cock through the fabric.

"What did I do?" Max protested.

"You took your shirt off." Blake squeezed Max's balls.

"Aagh! Blake, stop! I just wanted to feel the sun on my skin."

"Happy to oblige." Blake yanked Max's underwear down to his ankles where he could kick them free. "Mmm. Much better. Turn over."

Max rolled onto his stomach, relieved he could hide his flaming face. It was marginally less embarrassing to have his ass exposed in the open air than his genitals.

"It's a good job I packed the sunscreen," Blake commented. "Don't think I covered this bit of you earlier."

A cold splat on Max's ass was followed by Blake smoothing the lotion into his skin.

"Oh!" Max yelped as more of the cold cream was targeted at his crack.

"Open your legs wider," Blake ordered.

Max inched them apart, hyper-aware of his cock rubbing against the picnic blanket. Then Blake was pushing lotion into his hole and all he wanted was to be filled. The stretching Blake gave him was cursory to say the least. First two fingers, then three. Not rough but decisive. There were

137

clearly condoms packed in with the sandwiches and fruit because Max detected the distinct sound of foil ripping. Then Blake maneuvered him onto all fours and pressed into him. The angle was perfect. Blake pegged his prostate with every forceful thrust. Max's own keening cries filled his ears.

"That's it. Let me hear you. Tell me want you want, Max."

"Please, Sir. Let me come!" Max reached for his cock but Blake smacked his hand away.

"That's mine."

"No, please… I have to."

To Max's relief, Blake took a firm hold of his cock. He jacked him roughly, moving his hand in synchronization with the snapping of his hips.

"Please!" Max could hardly define what it was he wanted. He needed something… His body screamed at him…but subconsciously he recognized that only Blake could grant what he needed. His role was to take what Max gave him. He grunted at the jarring force of Blake's penetration. Blake pressed his nail into Max's slit.

"Come."

One word and his body responded, a hair trigger stroked into action. He fired his release into the blanket, frantically pushing into Blake's grip. He registered the exact moment that Blake came. A sudden moment of stillness followed by intense heat and a jubilant rush of endorphins. He had brought Blake to that precious point of ecstasy. A sense of power rushed through him along with the realization that as much as he had grown to need Blake, Blake needed him too. Max collapsed onto his belly and Blake followed him down, still inside him. He nibbled at Max's neck, making him giggle.

"Fucking you is going to become an addiction," Blake murmured.

"Beat you to it, Sir. I'm already hooked." Max squeezed Blake's cock with his inner muscles.

"Brat."

Blake bit the back of Max's neck hard enough to leave a bruise. It made Max think of a documentary he'd seen about pack dynamics—an alpha wolf exerting its dominance. He relaxed under Blake's weight, unresisting. When Blake eventually rolled off him, Max immediately missed the connection. He flopped onto his back and watched while Blake dealt with the condom. Then he used a napkin from the picnic basket to clean them both up a bit. He was still dressed and, after zipping up his jeans, was barely rumpled. Max reached for his discarded clothes.

"Oh no you don't." Blake threw the pile farther away. "I prefer you just the way you are." He straddled Max's body, settling against him.

Max remained still, enjoying the renewed closeness.

"I'm not crushing you, am I?" Blake asked.

They were pressed together from thigh to hip, Blake balancing on his elbows.

"Not at all. S'nice." Max wriggled, making himself more comfortable. The blanket beneath him was soft, cushioned by the grass beneath. He caught glimpses of the sky but Blake's face commanded his attention. The storm gray of his eyes seemed softer, more muted. Suddenly shy, Max didn't know what else to say. Then Blake kissed him and words became superfluous.

Max lost himself in the press of Blake's lips, the taste of him, the strength and control. Time ceased. Then Max's stomach rumbled and the spell was broken. Blake pulled away from the kiss and raised an eyebrow. Mortified, Max broke into uncontrolled giggles.

"Sorry!" He couldn't stop laughing.

Blake rolled his eyes. "So much for that romantic moment." He shifted away from Max to stretch out. "It's my fault. I nag you about eating properly then keep you from the food."

"For the best of reasons, Sir." Max would go hungry for the rest of the day if it meant more of Blake's kisses.

Blake traced a line from Max's collarbone to his navel.

139

"Let's eat. I intend to take full advantage of a rare day's freedom, and that means you need to keep your strength up."

"Yes, Sir." Max scrambled to his knees. He unloaded the contents of the basket onto the rug. Ada had packed silverware and china as well as a vast selection of food. Max's mouth watered at the sight of grilled chicken, Caesar salad, chilled salmon in a dill sauce and a host of savory and sweet nibbles. "Wow, this is an amazing spread!"

"Don't stand on ceremony. Dig in." Blake poured them both some chilled juice.

Max still waited for Blake to stack his plate before he took a bite himself. The food was so good, he could almost forget he was naked. Almost. It might have been easier if Blake didn't continually rake him with smoldering glances. Max began to wonder what Blake had planned. He drew his knees up and hugged them.

"Have you had enough to eat?" Blake asked.

There was a whole world of meaning in that line. If Max said yes, Blake's plans would be revealed. Max wasn't sure he could handle that. Of course, if he said no there would be no more kisses. That made the decision easy.

"Full to the brim." Max grinned. He hadn't meant it to sound like an innuendo.

"Good, because I can tell you're thinking too much. It's a habit I need to break you from."

Blake packed their picnic things away and dragged the rug to the base of a broad-leafed oak. He sat with his back to the tree and patted his lap. "Come here."

Catching the glint in Blake's eyes, Max rolled onto his knees and crawled over to Blake. He clambered onto Blake's lap, wishing his thighs could meet skin rather than denim.

"So, another first for you today," Blake said.

Max curled against him. "Several, actually."

"Tell me."

"Well, there was the whole outdoor sex thing." Max hid his face against Blake's shirt.

"There was." Blake lifted Max's chin. "No hiding. What else?"

"Picnicking naked."

"Something we should do often."

"But *we* implies you should be naked too." Max teased open the top button of Blake's shirt. He planted a soft kiss on the patch of skin he exposed.

"But then you wouldn't feel so deliciously vulnerable, would you?"

Blake made no objection as Max progressed to the next button.

"I have a couple of outdoor scenes we can try," Blake said.

Max froze. The hard ridge of Blake's cock pressed into his belly.

"You do?" His voice trembled. His dick jerked.

"I've always wondered what it would be like to fuck a man against a tree. Tie him there with thick ropes, dick pressed to the bark."

Max shifted in Blake's lap, his balls uncomfortably tight and hot. "Red maples have quite smooth bark..."

"Oh, they do? I'll bear that in mind." Blake cupped Max's ass. "Do you ever watch old pirate or cowboy films where the hero gets staked out on the ground?"

A whimper was all Max could manage by way of response.

"I'd like to drive some stakes into the grass, then tie you to them. Torment you a little with a soft flogger. Your cock would be as stiff as one of the stakes, wouldn't it?"

"Oh God."

"Then I'd release your ankles, bend you double and fuck you until you screamed."

"You have a vivid imagination, Sir." Max gulped.

"How about you? Do you have any fantasies inhabiting that creative mind of yours?"

Closing his eyes, Max thought about it. His imagination was usually confined to the possibilities of chemical reactions. "It doesn't really count as outdoors, but I had a dream once." He hesitated, images flooding his head.

"Go on."

"I'm in a barn. One of those really high, wooden ones. There are bales of hay everywhere... I can almost smell them. The sun is filtering through the wooden slats, casting stripes on the floor, and I can see dust motes dancing in the sunbeams."

"Is it warm?"

"Yes. Really warm. I'm suspended from a beam, naked, my toes just touching the ground. The sun is on my skin."

"I love the image so far. What happens next?"

"There's another man there. I can't see his face, but he's shirtless, holding a whip. I'm not afraid. I'm hard. I want him to use it."

"And does he?" Blake stroked Max's hair.

"I don't know. I woke up before the good part." Max sighed.

"There's a barn on the property here, you know. It's not huge, but it is a wooden one." Blake grinned. "Perhaps one day I'll make your dream come true."

Max squirmed, his cock rising. He petted the exposed part of Blake's chest. Blake dug in his pocket. He extracted a foil wrapped condom and a sachet of lube. "Don't think I haven't noticed your covert attempt to get me out of my clothes. Keep going and we'll make use of these."

Max tackled buttons and zips with renewed enthusiasm. Soon Blake was bared to the elements, Max kneeling across his thighs. He licked his lips, wondering if he dared ask for a taste.

"Much as I would love your sweet lips wrapped around my cock, sweetheart—I want to come inside you."

Max pouted. "How did you know what I was thinking?"

"Because you, my sweet innocent Max, are an open book. Glove me up then use the slick. Make sure to leave some for yourself."

Max rolled the gossamer sheath down Blake's straining shaft. He applied a coating of lube then reached back to apply the rest to his own hole. Tiny lines of tension appeared

142

around Blake's eyes.

"I could watch you do that for hours," Blake muttered. "But I want to see you ride me. Hands behind your back." He grasped Max's hips, nudging him into the correct position. "I'd prefer them tied, so consider yourself bound by my words."

Fingers locked together, Max made no attempt to control his movement. Blake held him safe, guided him. The plump head of Blake's cock breached his entrance with ease. Steady pressure from Blake, assisted by gravity, soon had Max seated in his lap fully impaled. Max panted, getting accustomed to the stretch and slight burn. He pinched his lower lip between his teeth.

"So full." The words came out as a gasp.

Blake flicked one of Max's nipples. The sting shot straight from his chest to his groin. His cock twitched. He wanted to move but Blake was holding him still, pinning him in place.

"Next time." Blake flicked his nipple harder. "I'd enjoy seeing you moan around a gag."

He tormented the same nipple over and over until Max writhed in his grasp. When Max thought he couldn't take it anymore, Blake lifted him then allowed him to drop. Max screamed. He grabbed one wrist with his other hand and squeezed in the hope that more pain would prevent him from coming untouched and without permission.

"Fuck yourself on me," Blake growled, his eyes glassy.

Max bucked and slid, the movements jerky and uncoordinated. He needed Blake deeper. He was close, so close. Teetering on the edge of orgasm. Blake smacked Max's cock with his open palm. Fire shot to his balls and he came in an unstoppable gush, spraying Blake's abs. Before he could recover, Blake lifted him free as if he weighed nothing. He flipped Max over onto all fours and spanked him hard—six stinging slaps that brought him to a climax for the second time, wringing him dry.

Resting his forehead on the ground, Max sobbed from the intensity of it. Blake drove into him, pushing deep. A few snaps of his hips, then the warm gush of heat as the condom filled. Max pushed back, grinding against Blake's groin, determined to squeeze every ounce of pleasure from him. Blake stilled and Max wished he could see the rictus of ecstasy that he assumed to be fixing Blake's expression. After one final push and a satisfied grunt, Blake slid free of Max's grasping channel and collapsed next to him on the rug. Max slumped onto his belly, breathing hard. His ass burned. He had to roll over because his cock was so sensitive he couldn't bear contact with the rug.

"Back to zero," Blake said.

"Sorry?" Max couldn't make his brain work.

"You've paid off your debt for swearing."

"Oh! But I owed you five, Sir, not six."

"I added one because you came without permission."

Max gave him an incredulous stare. "You... But there was no way... I mean, it was your fault I came, Sir."

"It was."

Blake leaned over him.

"Your point is?"

Max parted his lips in invitation. Blake accepted. He ravished Max's mouth with a kiss that left him gasping, lips throbbing. All thoughts of protest evacuated his brain.

"Put your hands above your head."

It was hard to control his limp arms, but Max managed. Blake gripped both his wrists in one hand, then kissed him again. This time the contact was soft, almost chaste. Max hummed his pleasure. The pressure on his wrists left him in no doubt as to who was in charge. It satisfied his deep need to be cared for, owned. A need he was just beginning to accept.

# Chapter Thirteen

In his head, Max was chained to Blake's bed, his legs held wide apart by a spreader bar. How he'd loved having his choices taken away. The spider gag holding his mouth open for Blake to fuck had been a devilish touch. His jaw had ached for hours afterward. That weekend spent learning about Blake's kinks and fantasies had been a revelation, as Max's own desires had been dragged into the light. Blake had been patient but persistent, metaphorically holding his hand every passionate inch of the way.

"What are you looking so smug about, Mr. Allenby?"

Ella Preston surely had acid instead of saliva in that cruel mouth of hers. Max held back a sigh and attempted to appear less happy. He pressed his lips together in a tight line and frowned, directing his ire at his computer screen. Even Dr. Preston's baiting couldn't dampen his mood, though she was doing her very best to wear him down. Knowing that he would be going home to Blake got him through even the worst days. He caught a sympathetic glance from Sara, one of the lab technicians, and gave her a rueful smile. Ella Preston was a bully through and through, using her position to cover her own inadequacies. Max bore the brunt of her vitriol but that didn't mean his colleagues got away with easy lives. They all had to deal with the bitch boss from hell.

"I'm presenting the research paper on the new polymer compound to the board this afternoon. When I get back I expect all last week's data to be entered and the analysis program started." Dr. Preston leaned over Max's shoulder and he thought he detected a hint of alcohol on her breath.

"It looks to me as if you'll need to work late again tonight."

Max didn't respond in case he said something he'd regret. She was right, though. There was no way he'd be able to input all his data without working well into the night. He had worked late every day for the last two weeks. There was always something he had 'forgotten' or experiments that had mysteriously become corrupted and needed repeating. It had only been a short while since he'd spent the weekend with Blake, and Max's Dom was not impressed that their time together was reduced. He had offered to step in but Max wanted to deal with the problem himself. Facing up to the bullying was something he had to do on his own.

Dr. Preston grabbed her jacket and swung around to leave. A sleeve caught the pot of paperclips on Max's desk. It went flying and the clips created silver rain, shooting and skidding into every nook and cranny of the lab as they hit the floor.

"Oh dear. I imagine it will take you quite a while to pick those up," Dr. Preston said, satisfaction dripping from every word. The awful woman flounced out of the door without a backward glance.

Max raked trembling fingers through his hair, clambered off his stool and started to collect the scattered clips. One of his colleagues immediately came to join him.

"The old bat has really got it in for you, Max. What's her problem?" Jenny, one of the research assistants, patted his shoulder. "Sooner or later someone's going to realize that you're the one that does all the work around here. You have more talent in your pinkie than she does in her entire obnoxious body. Can I get you a coffee?"

Max shrugged. "You work hard too, we're a team. It's not just me, and I've no idea what I've done to make Dr. Preston dislike me so much." He always felt a bit tongue-tied around his colleagues, especially Jenny, who tended to mother him.

As the only man in the lab, he kept quiet rather than make an idiot of himself. Two of the girls had made unsubtle passes at him after he'd arrived and he'd had to confess he was gay rather than hurt their feelings. Now all they did was try to set him up with prospective boyfriends. They had absolutely no idea he was dating the owner of the company and if Max had his way, they never would. Blake was content to be open, but Max didn't want his colleagues hating him because they thought he got special favors from the boss.

"I think she's intimidated by your intellect. The science comes easily to you. If she could absorb your brainpower, she would. Soul-sucking zombie."

"I think zombies suck brains, Jenny. Not sure who goes after souls—vampires maybe?" He smiled. "But I appreciate the support. It means a lot. I'd love a coffee, if you don't mind getting them while I finish hunting down these little beggars." Max fished some paperclips from behind the bin. He could have just left them where they'd fallen but inevitably someone would slip on one and hurt themselves. The tiled floor of the lab was not a comfortable place to land. If Ella Preston were to take a tumble he wouldn't object, but with her charmed life it would more likely be him testing the bounce qualities of his rear.

"Okay, sweetie, won't be long."

Max heaved a sigh of relief as Jenny left him to it. He knelt up, easing a slight cramp in his back, and chuckled. In the last couple of weeks, he'd spent quite a lot of time on his knees, but in significantly more pleasurable activity. "Oh God, not now!" he muttered under his breath. Thinking about sucking Blake off had an inevitable effect on Max's cock. He scrambled to his feet and buttoned his lab coat all the way to the bottom. Fortunately it was two sizes bigger than he needed and hid a multitude of sins.

He finished retrieving all the clips he could see, then sat in front of his computer and stared at the screen, willing the figures there to make some kind of sense. His concentration was shot to pieces. He and Blake had agreed to keep their relationship out of the workplace but Max couldn't block it from his mind. Blake was quite happy for him to be independent. He didn't have to ask permission to do anything. Blake was very strict when they spent time together but applied no pressure for Max to behave any differently than he had before they were a couple. The trouble was, Max found that he didn't like having so much freedom. When he and Blake were apart he felt lost—not incapable or less intelligent, just a bit detached from reality. Blake was a grounding force in his life, filling a hole that he hadn't even realized was there. Much as he hated to admit it, he relaxed more when he had an order to follow.

Max ground his teeth, his nerves shot to pieces. Ella Preston was off presenting a paper *he* had written, no doubt passing it off as her own. He had invested blood, sweat and tears in its production. Tears of frustration when things went wrong—bucketloads of sweat as he'd tested pieces of prototype body armor in extreme conditions and real, red blood when an exploding test tube had almost taken his eye out one afternoon. He had a tiny scar on his cheekbone as a reminder of that incident. He might not get the credit for the work but he was still too invested in it not to care about the outcome of the afternoon's presentation, and it was inevitable that his boss would do a half-assed job.

The internal messenger box pinged up on his screen, and he minimized it quickly as a sixth sense detected Jenny coming up behind him. She deposited a cup of ridiculously strong coffee on the desk next to him.

"There you go, sweetie. Black with two sugars."

"Thanks, Jenny, that should keep me awake for the rest of the week." He gave her a grateful smile.

"You're too young to sleep anyway. I don't believe in that wishy washy milky stuff. Coffee should put hairs on your chest." She winked then sashayed back to her own desk across the room.

Max took a gulp of the coffee, trying to bleach the image of a hairy-chested Jenny from his mind. He brought the messenger system back up, his heart pounding.

*Are you being good?*

The message was from Blake, breaking his own rules as he did every day. Max mulled over what to type back, knowing that his words could have unexpected impact.

*Not really.*

He held his breath.

*You know what that means.*

Max knew exactly what it meant. So did his cock, which jerked enthusiastically.

*Tell me.*

The cursor flashed forever.

*Use your imagination.*

*No fair.*

*D-Day. Gotta go.*

The box closed. Max chewed on his bottom lip and ducked his head. He didn't dare catch anyone's eye because he was absolutely certain he would give himself away. He blushed far too easily, something Blake teased him about constantly. Blake—just the man's name sent shivers down Max's spine. He squirmed on his stool and resorted to sipping more of Jenny's terrible coffee. It was an important day. His paper could secure the future of Armacom. He should be obsessing more about that and less about Blake's plans for that night.

Knowing that Blake would be tied up at the board meeting for a couple of hours allowed Max a modicum of concentration. Otherwise, he would be constantly hoping that Blake might pay an unscheduled visit to the lab. He immersed himself in his work and gradually the outside world faded away. Chemical formulae were safe and unthreatening. He felt comfortable with complex problems—it was a world he could hide in. He typed at high speed, his screen filling with a table of figures and notes of his thoughts.

When his phone rang an hour later, Max nearly fell off his stool. It took him a while to work out what was happening but he eventually managed to pull together enough composure to pick up the handset. It was Amanda, Blake's fearsome personal assistant. Max found himself sitting up straighter. Amanda knew everything about everyone and probably had surveillance cameras in the lab. She'd know if he was slouching.

"Max, you're wanted in the boardroom." Amanda sounded as cool and calm as always. Max had been upgraded from a coldly formal 'Mr. Allenby' to his first name since Amanda had surmised that he and Blake were together.

"What—*now*?" Max stuttered into the phone. It was too soon. The board meeting couldn't be that far along. It usually took them an hour or more to get through the preliminaries, minutes of the previous meeting and brief departmental updates. His paper wasn't scheduled to be on the agenda until near the end.

"No, a fortnight Thursday." Sarcasm oozed through Amanda's every word.

Max could imagine her shaking her immaculately coiffured head in despair at his idiocy.

"They moved your paper up the agenda to allow for more discussion time and there's some kind of problem with it. I don't have any more information than that. Just get yourself over here quick smart."

"On my way. Do I need to bring anything with me?"

"No. Just flatten your hair a bit, you no doubt resemble a baby hedgehog." She rang off.

150

Heart pounding, Max ripped off his lab coat and checked his tie for coffee stains—thankfully it was clean. He didn't have a jacket with him, but his shirt wasn't too rumpled, though it did have an ink stain on the pocket. He caught Jenny's curious glance and mouthed the word *boardroom* across at her.

"Oh my God!" She marched across the room and started manhandling him, tightening the knot on his tie then fetching him a comb from her voluminous handbag. "Try and do something with that mop, Maxie—you look like a surfer, not a scientist."

"Does every woman in this building have an opinion about my hair?" Max grumbled.

"Of course we do," Jenny said as if he was an idiot to even imply that they didn't have an automatic right to criticize every aspect of his appearance. She marched back to her desk.

He dragged the instrument of torture through his tangled locks with a grimace, grateful that Jenny hadn't attempted to do it for him. It wouldn't have surprised him. He gave up on his hair and tossed the comb down on his desk. "That will have to do." He grabbed a pen and a notepad then ran for the door, trying not to panic.

By the time he'd crossed the building he was a little calmer, if out of breath. Amanda didn't give him any time to make excuses.

She gave him a critical examination. "You'll do." She picked a piece of lint from his shoulder then opened the boardroom door.

Max froze. "My legs have stopped working," he whispered.

"In." Amanda gave him a gentle shove.

Max stumbled across the threshold then stood just inside the door. He took in the group around the table. Eleven seats were occupied, the twelfth stood empty. Blake was holding court at the head of the table.

"Ah, Mr. Allenby. Thank you for joining us," Blake said.

"I'm hoping that you might be able to shed some light on a little problem we have with the polymer paper."

Max took a couple of shaky steps forward. It was only Blake's encouraging smile that stopped his knees from buckling completely. "I don't understand. There's a problem? I checked all the data myself."

"Dr. Preston here" — Blake gestured to Max's stony-faced boss seated to Blake's left — "has just made a competent job of presenting the paper." Blake managed to make 'competent' sound like the most insulting word in the English language. "However, as several of our board members have pointed out, the analysis is utter garbage and makes no sense whatsoever. Dr. Preston seems unable to offer an explanation other than that she put *her* name to a paper written by *you* and therefore the incompetence is yours."

Blake walked the length of the table and pressed a copy of the offending document into Max's hand. Their fingers brushed and that slight contact gave Max the confidence he needed. He looked at the first few pages of the paper.

"Oh! I'm very sorry, Mr. Winters — it *is* my mistake. It seems I must have given Dr. Preston the security copy of the paper instead of the real one. I can only apologize." He glued his gaze to the carpet and shuffled his feet, doing his best impression of a scatterbrained geek.

"Explain please, for the board." Blake's voice was hard as stone.

"Sorry, Sir. Of course." Max gulped. He wouldn't ever want to be on Blake's bad side. He scanned the unsmiling faces of Armacom's board members. "Here at Armacom we have a security protocol that dictates false versions of all secret work must be made and placed on the servers. They are more easily accessible on the computer system than the genuine articles, which have additional layers of password protection — it's to cut down on the risk of hackers stealing valuable proprietary information. I can retrieve the correct paper in seconds — perhaps I could use your office computer, Mr. Winters?"

"Mr. Allenby, allow me to introduce myself." A silver-haired man in an immaculate charcoal suit stepped away from the table and extended his hand.

Max shook it, hoping that his palms weren't too clammy.

"Professor Geoff Palmer, Chairman of the Board."

"How do you do, sir. It's very nice to meet you." Max knew exactly who the esteemed professor was, he had read all of his published work.

"And you, Mr. Allenby. Perhaps you could clarify the situation for me. From what you've said, my understanding is that not only did Dr. Preston fraudulently put her own name on *your* work, she was too inept to notice that it was the wrong version?"

Max didn't say a word. He didn't trust himself to speak. His silence was telling enough. A low hum of urgent conversation filled the room. Blake picked up the phone and dialed a single digit.

"Amanda, please ask security to attend the boardroom and advise them that Dr. Preston is to be escorted from the building."

Dr. Preston's gasp of indignation should have been funny but Max didn't feel much like laughing.

"You can't do that! I have a contract." Ella Preston's face was the color of beetroot.

"Actually, I believe I can." Blake looked to the board members for endorsement and got a unanimous round of nods. "Your actions constitute gross misconduct. I will have security forward any personal possessions to your home address. Needless to say, references will not be provided. My only regret is that it has taken this long to uncover your ineptitude."

Dr. Preston stood up and shoved her chair back, toppling it. She pointed at Max. "You! You planned this all along, you little fairy!" She stormed down the room toward Max. She raised her hand.

Max cowered back against the wall but just as his soon to

153

be ex boss was about to strike him the door slammed open and Justin, along with two uniformed security guards, thundered in. Max had never been so glad to see his brother's determined face. Ella Preston was efficiently restrained and hauled out of the room by Justin's colleagues, shouting and cursing in a very unladylike fashion. Max sagged against the wall, which was the only thing holding him up. He took a few deep breaths.

"Jesus, Max, what the hell have you been up to?" Justin scowled. He pulled Max out of the room then placed his hands on Max's shoulders.

"Why do you automatically assume it's me that's been up to something?" Max whined, trying to catch sight of Blake over Justin's solid frame. "And shouldn't you be helping your team?"

"They can cope without me, and to answer your first question — a lifetime of experience and a childhood pulling you out of scrapes caused by your mad experiments."

"Wow, you have a selective memory. I recall you being the one that got *me* into trouble all the time."

Justin shrugged. "All those chemicals you work with have rotted your brain. Are you okay? What's going on?"

"I'm good. A bit shaky, that's all. Dr. Preston didn't touch me." He targeted a beseeching look at Blake.

"You can let go of him, Justin, he's not going to fall apart," Blake said, stepping out of the boardroom to join them.

Justin took a single pace back. "If you say so." He peered from Blake to Max then back again. "Is one of you going to clue me in here?"

Blake chuckled. He grabbed Max's hand and shook it. "Well done. That was an Oscar winning performance. You even had me convinced."

Max smiled shyly. He desperately wanted Blake to pull him into a hug, but it wasn't going to happen where there were so many potential witnesses. The boardroom door was open and Max caught a couple of curious glances being sent their way.

"I'm confused," Justin complained.

"Max and I cooked up a little plot to trap Ella Preston into revealing how she'd been stealing Max's work and it just paid off," Blake explained.

"You did? That bat has had it coming to her for a while. She's a nasty piece of work."

"The bat, as you so accurately call her, proved to be very good at covering her tracks," Blake said. "It was your security system that helped catch her out in the end, but it took some great acting from Max. He had to make her believe she had the correct paper, when what she actually had was a fake."

"It's been a hairy couple of weeks," Max said. "She's had ages to prepare for today and I was convinced she'd spot the fake paper before now. The analysis in it was utter garbage. Fortunately she was true to form and didn't prepare properly. I just gave her a few crib notes and told her to reference the presentation slides, which I'd also put together. She knew enough about the work to think she could get away with winging it." Max giggled, a bit hysterical. "I need a drink."

"Oh no you don't," Blake said. "You know what happened the last time you resorted to alcohol."

Max blinked. He remembered exactly how that had turned out. His cock jerked.

Justin shook his head. "Blake's right. You have no capacity for alcohol whatsoever. I remember your twenty-first birthday when you ended up dancing naked down—"

"Justin! Shut up!" Max clamped a hand over his brother's mouth.

"Interesting," Blake said. "You and I will have to get together for a chat about Max's youthful antics, Justin."

Justin pushed Max's hand away from his mouth. "That will be a pleasure, but for now I have to go and deal with our ex member of staff. Little brother, you and I are going to have a serious conversation about this sometime soon." He strolled away, after giving Max a final pat on the back.

155

"You holding up okay?" Blake asked. He stood in front of Max, blocking him from the view of the milling board members, some of whom were starting to spill from the boardroom.

"My legs are jelly. I'd rather be walking on broken glass than in this room. Public speaking of any kind induces spectacular projectile vomiting in me, but yeah, I'm fine." Max gazed longingly at the fire exit and wondered if he could make a run for it.

"I'll position the trash can within range." Blake squeezed his arm. "You'll do fine. I'm proud of you." He herded everyone back into the boardroom. "Well, ladies and gentlemen." Blake addressed the group. "I suggest we break for coffee while the correct papers are copied and then Mr. Allenby can present *his* work."

Much chatter ensued. Max thought it was probably the most exciting thing that had happened in the boardroom since the day someone had knocked a cup of coffee over their laptop and fused the electrics.

He stuck to the safety of a position against the wall. To his relief, Blake brought him a glass of water rather than coffee.

"Thanks." He took the glass and sipped.

"After what you just said, I didn't think coffee was advisable," Blake said with a grin. "You're quite the actor, aren't you? You pulled off the whole sweet and innocent thing beautifully."

"I *am* sweet and innocent." Max fluttered his lashes and gave him a coy glance.

Blake snorted. "You're a brat, and far too clever for your own good."

Max attempted to look angelic. "Yes, Sir. Whatever you say."

Blake rolled his eyes, but he was smiling. "Just wait till I get you home."

Max swallowed and wished he could loosen his tie. He was getting harder and there was no lab coat to hide his condition. "Hush, someone will hear you."

"You may want to consider sitting down to deliver your presentation, Max." Blake smirked. "I'm going to get myself a drink and mingle a bit. Why don't you go and get a copy of the correct paper from Amanda and sit outside until we're ready for you?"

Max shot out of the room like his pants were on fire. Amanda grabbed him as he ran past her desk, stopping him dead.

"Where do you think you're going? You have a paper to present." She pushed him down into a chair.

"I didn't sign up for this, Amanda. I'm a scientist. I belong in a lab, not the boardroom."

"Stick your head between your knees and take a few deep breaths."

Max took her advice but it didn't help much. At least he didn't have to look at anyone.

Amanda handed him a sheaf of papers. "You don't want to let Blake down, do you? He's relying on you."

"I know." Max leaned forward again in an attempt to reduce his nausea. "You've found my weak spot. There's not much I wouldn't do for him."

"Think of it like this, in an hour it will all be over and you can go hide in the lab. Oh, I think they're ready for you. Either that or Blake's waving for exercise."

Max giggled. "Thanks, Amanda. You rock. Wish me luck." With his heart in his mouth, he made his way back into the boardroom.

* * * *

Blake lounged on the couch and sipped the single glass of wine he had allowed himself. The crisp pinot grigio was a treat. He was very careful about how much he drank, especially when he played with Max, but this glass was well deserved. He sighed, contentment settling deep in his bones. The day had gone extraordinarily well. The thorn in his side that was Ella Preston had been extracted. Max had given an endearing performance in front of the board, and Blake's funding options had been unanimously endorsed. He smiled. If it had been anyone but Max, he might have thought the shaking hands and nervous looks as he read his paper were an act, but it was clear to everyone present that Max was terrified. It had taken all Blake's self-control not to comfort him. After the meeting, when Max had scurried away to the safety of his lab, the chairman of the board had shaken Blake's hand firmly.

"This work will secure the future of Armacom for a long time to come, Blake. Congratulations, you have quite a find there."

"Thanks, Geoff. The investment will pay off, I'm sure," Blake had said.

"I'm certain it will, but I'm not talking about the polymer project, I'm referring to your young scientist. Quite a prodigy." Geoff had given a deep chuckle. "I hope you're looking after him? We wouldn't want to lose him to the competition."

For once Blake had been lost for words. He'd given his friend a hard look. "What exactly do you mean by *my* scientist?"

"Blake, if you want to keep your relationship secret, you'll need to tell young Max not to look at you like you're the only person in the room. That young man adores you. It's as obvious as the nose on my face. Tell me I'm wrong but I don't think it has anything to do with hero worship."

"He... I... Oh, to hell with it. Yes, we're together, and yes, I am looking after him." He'd waited for something to happen. The room had suddenly got much quieter.

"Well, it's about time you found someone. Keep a tight hold of that one, he's a keeper!"

The slap on his back that had followed had propelled Blake forward a couple of steps. He'd glanced around and caught a few pleased smiles before people had turned back to their own conversations. He just hoped that relationship updates wouldn't become a standing item on board agendas.

158

Max was shivering again at that moment but Blake hoped it was from anticipation rather than nerves. His position was perfect as he knelt naked on the hearthrug, his hands bound behind his back with soft, red rope. A simple red leather cock ring held his rigid erection proud from his body and a stiff posture collar held his head up. There would be no staring at the floor tonight.

Blake unzipped his fly and released his straining cock. It felt hot and hard in his hand as he wrapped his fingers around it and gave it a few careful strokes. There was no way he wanted to come until he was buried deep in Max's sweet ass, and he was already close.

Max whimpered, the sound a plea for attention.

"You're irresistible. I could sit here and stare at you for hours." Blake shifted forward until he was at the edge of the couch. He spread his legs a little wider. "Come and stand here, love." He pointed to a spot between his knees.

Max clambered awkwardly to his feet and took a couple of paces forward. His dick was at the perfect height for Blake's mouth. Blake abandoned his own cock in favor of Max's. He rubbed the gleaming head with the pad of his thumb and flicked Max's balls hard enough to sting. Max's gasp of pleasure almost made Blake come. A wry shake of his head acknowledged his lack of control. He leaned forward to lick the gleaming droplet of pre-cum that had gathered at the head of Max's cock. He kissed the gleaming tip then took the plump crown into his mouth. Just the crown, nothing more. He palmed Max's ass, locked his elbows for more stability and started to suck hard. The muscles beneath his fingers tensed into hardness and Max let out a little yelp. Blake grinned and swirled his tongue around before biting gently.

"Oh! Oh, Sir! Please! I need to come... Oh God!"

Blake let Max's cock slide from between his lips with some regret. "Turn around and bend over." He snapped the words out harshly, his own need making him impatient.

Max turned and bent at the waist, presenting Blake with

159

a beautiful view of his ass. His bound hands rested at the small of his back, fingers fluttering in agitation. Blake grabbed Max's slim hips and pulled him back a little. "Spread your legs wider. I've got you, I won't let you fall."

There, that was better. The position exposed Max's cute little hole nicely. Blake didn't hesitate. He blew a stream of air onto the puckered skin then licked around the edge. Max jerked in his grip, and Blake dug his fingers in harder, holding him still. Max would no doubt have bruises the next day but that was no bad thing. Blake liked having his marks on Max's pristine skin. Without warning, he plunged his tongue into moist warmth, tasting and probing. Max screamed and Blake had to tense his arms to hold Max's weight. He took his time and tortured Max a while longer, exploring his channel as deeply as he could.

When Max began to sob and beg for mercy, Blake relented. He grabbed the lube from the arm of the sofa and squeezed some onto his fingers. Max started to straighten up so Blake gave him a firm slap, then watched in delight as rosy pink spread across Max's smooth ass.

"No. You stay bent over until I say you can move." Blake smeared lube around Max's entrance then deftly slipped a finger into welcoming warmth.

He didn't wait long before adding a second digit but moved slowly, checking for any sign of discomfort from Max. The fact that Max was squirming like an eel and pushing back hard against him gave him all the reassurance he needed. He twisted his fingers then crooked them together, seeking and finding the spongy bundle of nerves that triggered such pleasure. Max squealed and tremors ran through his body. He seemed to be having a hard time staying on his feet.

Carefully, Blake withdrew his fingers. He gave Max's ass a pat. "Turn around and face me, you can straighten up now."

Max did as he'd been told. His face was flushed and his eyes bright, his cheeks streaked with tears. His breath was coming in short, sharp gasps. Blake unbuttoned his shirt with slow, deliberate movements, then removed it. Then he slipped off his pants and underwear and kicked them aside. It felt good to be naked, the air cooling his overheated skin. He sat back and played with his dick a little, never breaking eye contact with Max. He grabbed a condom packet, tore it open and applied the rubber in one smooth motion. Then he squeezed more glistening gel from the tube and spread it over his gloved shaft, watching as Max's eyes widened.

"Come here, sweetheart." Blake put his hands around Max's trim waist and pulled him into position so that he straddled Blake's thighs. "Now kneel on the couch and take me inside you. You're in charge. I'll hold you in place, you won't fall."

Max looked at him with trepidation. "But, Sir... You're so... It's so... I can't!"

Blake laughed and stroked a hand over Max's ass, trying to calm him. "You do my ego the power of good, boy, but believe me, you can and you will. You've taken me plenty of times before."

"Yes, but that was with you in control. This way it's me."

"No. I'm ordering you to do it. You will submit and obey." Max needed to know that Blake still orchestrated his pleasure.

Max clambered on to the sofa, spreading his thighs wide, balancing on his knees. Blake gripped his waist, knowing that with his hands bound Max could do nothing to save himself if he overbalanced.

Tentatively, Max raised himself up then lowered back down. There was a moment's resistance as the head of Blake's cock hit Max's entrance, but then it slipped inside. Max was so warm and tight. They were a perfect fit. Max tried to keep his movement slow but gravity was not his friend and he dropped hard onto Blake's lap with a gasp that was part pleasure, part pain. Blake rocked him gently as Max got accustomed to the new position and the stretch of Blake's cock inside him.

Blake remembered that he had to breathe in order to

stay alive. He didn't want to come too soon but having his beautiful boy impaled on his dick was testing his self-control to the limit.

"Ride me. I want to see you pleasuring yourself."

Max's eyes got impossibly wider but he obeyed. Just a little at first, he raised himself up an inch then dropped back. Blake grunted at the friction. It felt incredible. Blake kept him steady but made no other attempt to control Max's movements. Gradually, Max got bolder, lifting and descending with increasing speed, getting higher until Blake's dick almost slipped from his body before he plunged back down again. His skin gleamed with a sheen of sweat. His lips parted.

"Eyes on me, Max." The collar he wore didn't allow Max to hide. His bound cock strained against its leather ring. Blake flicked the stud to release it and Max cried out.

"Please, Sir. I have to come. I can't stop it."

"You can. You don't have my permission yet." Blake took control. He held Max down, keeping him in his lap.

He pinched a nipple, twisting it until Max cried out. When he was sure that Max could keep his orgasm at bay a bit longer, he lifted him, then, as he dropped, Blake bucked his hips up, slamming them together. Max gasped, swore then began to mutter incomprehensible words through clenched teeth. Blake loved the position—it allowed him to get so deep and apply considerable force while still keeping Max safe. A few more snaps of his hips and he couldn't hold on any longer. He held Max's writhing body down and let his orgasm rip through him. As his shudders subsided a little, he encircled Max's erection with tight fingers and stroked. "Come for me, Max."

Max shot hard and fast, screaming Blake's name and splattering his body with ribbons of cum. Blake pulled Max against his chest and released his wrists. Max flung both arms around him with a shuddering sob.

"Sorry! Sorry... I don't know why I'm crying... It's just so good!"

Blake held Max tight as he snuggled into his neck. "As long as I didn't hurt you?"

"No! It was amazing… Incredible." Max leaned back and looked at Blake anxiously.

"Let's get that collar off, shall we?" Blake unbuckled the stiff leather and cast it aside.

Max rolled his neck in relief.

"Sore?" Blake checked for any abraded skin.

"No, just a bit of an ache. It was kind of hot." Max grinned.

"It certainly was." Blake kissed him. Max's lips were irresistible. He was soft and yielding, opening willingly. So beautifully, perfectly submissive. Still kissing, Blake stood, lifting Max with him. He allowed his cock to slide free from the warmth of Max's body then put him down on the sofa.

"I'll just be a moment." He covered Max with a soft throw.

Blake headed for the bathroom to clean up and dispose of the condom. When he returned with a warm washcloth, Max was curled into the corner of the couch looking thoroughly and happily sated. When Blake peeled back the throw, Max scowled and grumbled.

"Don't take my warm cuddly away."

"You're all sticky. Let me clean you up. And stop being a brat."

Max pouted prettily. Blake rolled his eyes. "Your new-found confidence is going to get you in all kinds of trouble!"

Max squirmed as Blake washed him. "I don't know what you mean?"

"That innocent act won't work on me, love. After today, I have no doubt there's a ruthless streak beneath that sweet exterior." He got under the throw and pulled Max into his lap. "I just wonder how you're going to get your own back on Justin now you've dealt with Ella Preston. You should show him some mercy, though — he did help to bring us together."

Max snickered. "Not a chance and I've already dealt with my big brother."

Blake slid his hand across Max's chest until he found a

perky nipple to pinch. "Tell me what you've done, or I'll tie you to the bed and stick a vibrating plug up your ass for the night!"

Max fluttered his eyelashes. "Is that a threat or a promise?"

Blake pinched him again. "Tell me!"

"Fine. You know the poster that depicts the stages of man's evolution? The one that starts with the ape and progresses to human?"

"Of course." Blake could not imagine where this conversation was heading.

"Well, I made a new version using pictures of Justin. Naked pictures. Naked baby Justin. Naked Justin in the paddling pool. Naked Justin on the beach. Bare-assed Justin on a stag do…"

Blake chuckled at the thought. "Wicked boy."

"Then I printed posters and put them up in the staff restaurant. Oh, and on Monday morning, everyone at Armacom is going to have a new screensaver on their computer."

Blake dissolved. "Justin's going to kill you! Then he's going to want you fired!"

Max wriggled back against Blake, getting as close as possible. "I think I'll be okay. The boss is in love with me. He'll protect me."

"Oh, will he indeed?"

"Uh-huh."

Blake jerked as Max squeezed his cock beneath the blanket.

"Well, the boss may well be head over heels in love with you, but that doesn't mean he's going to let you get away with murder." Blake surged to his feet and slung Max over his shoulder in a fireman's lift.

"Hey! Put me down!"

Blake gave Max's bare ass a sharp smack and ignored his protests. "This is self-preservation at work, boy. If I spank you now I can tell my head of security that you've been dealt with appropriately, and he won't inconveniently lose the keys to the executive bathroom."

Blake lugged Max upstairs then tossed his burden onto the bed and watched him sprawl in an ungainly tangle of limbs and sheets. Max sorted himself out and leaned back on his elbows with a very tempting smile. For a moment, Blake stood and just admired him. He had so many plans for his beautiful sub.

"Do your worst, Sir." Max began to stroke his hardening dick and gave him a challenging grin. He was utterly bewitching.

Blake faked a pained sigh. "I believe it's time to remind you exactly who is in charge."

STR**O**KE
RATE

*L. M. SOMERTON*

*LUCIEN LIKES TO
BE IN CONTROL*

# Stroke Rate

## *Excerpt*

## Chapter One

The October sun had dipped below the horizon some time since, and the distinct nip of autumn pervaded the air. The river was a black silk ribbon twisting sinuously toward the distant lights of the town—not really that far away but it could have been another world. The silence of the riverbank was broken only by the whisper of long grass and the occasional splash of a coot diving for cover amid the reeds.

It was the commotion of a startled bird that broke the reverie of the young man standing in the darkness. He gently flipped the small, smooth pebble that he had been turning over and over in his hand into the water. The resulting ripples caught the light reflected from the window of the building behind him. A slight smile flickered across his soft lips as he mused on the consequences that one small action could invoke. He sighed and turned away from the water. It had been a while since anything – or anyone – had created ripples in the monotony of his life.

A few steps took him to a low door that was slightly ajar, with warm light spilling around the edges as if trying to illuminate the night. At six feet tall, he had to duck his head as he slipped inside and pulled the door closed behind him. The small door he had used was cut into a much larger set that took up the whole wall. He breathed in the familiar smell of the boathouse. The wooden Edwardian structure had a smell all its own – oils and varnish mixed with the more modern scents of neoprene and acrylic paint, overlaid by the light fragrance of cedar and oak.

Okeanos Rowing Club owned an impressive set of immaculate boats that were racked along the walls. One full side stored the 'sweep' boats, where each rower has one oar. There were three eight-seaters and a range of single, double and quad boats all cradled by sturdy metal frames that could be cranked up the walls to provide more storage capacity. On the other side were the 'sculling' boats, which were all single and double seat arrangements. At the far end of the shed there was a trailer, pre-loaded with racing kayaks. They always had to be transported to other venues, so they stayed on their trailer, ready to go. The general equipment store could be reached through another door, and there were also two changing rooms with basic shower facilities at the back of the building.

Benedict Astor contemplated the view. Everything was in place, as it should be. Of course it was – after all, he was the one who had heaved and shoved every sodding boat into position, just as he had done virtually every night for the last six months. He rolled his shoulders and rubbed his aching arms before wandering over to the notice board to read the roughly scrawled note pinned there.

*Ben,*

*Extra jobs for tonight – clean the drain in the men's locker room, sand the front step (it's splintering again) and refill the water coolers.*

*S.*

"Just wonderful," Ben muttered quietly.

That was another hour's work at least, and it was already late. Ben used his long, slim fingers to tease at the knots in his collar-length hair before kneading away the tension in his tight neck muscles. He had an idea why Sebastian Cooke, the rowing club's president, had it in for him—but he wasn't sure, and it certainly wasn't something he was prepared to discuss with the man. It was easier just to put up with the never-ending list of menial tasks and hard labor that Seb took great delight in sending his way.

He tackled the worst job first, donning rubber gloves to remove the locker room drain cover and pull out the accumulated muck. He managed not to gag too much at the smell, then dumped half a bottle of bleach down the hole. The locker room now smelled like the inside of a hospital but even that was a distinct improvement. After replacing the plastic grating over the drain he peeled off the gloves and dumped them in the mop bucket. Next, he heaved three water bottles for the coolers out of the storage cupboard and replaced the half-empty ones, even though they didn't really need changing. Finally, he got down on his hands and knees and applied a piece of coarse sandpaper to the front step. Rowers, including him, often carried the boats back up from the river with bare feet, so this was one job he didn't mind doing. He'd gotten a splinter in his heel once and it had been not only uncomfortable, but also difficult to get out.

The sanding was strangely therapeutic, if hard on his fingers, and it gave him time to wonder—for the thousandth time—if the job was really worth it. He came to the same conclusion he always did. It was temporary. It wouldn't be forever, and three hours of labor a day wasn't a big price to pay for free accommodation and club membership. The tiny flat above the boat room wasn't much, but it was quiet and private, plus he could cycle along the riverside path to get to the university each day. Even at student rates there was no way he would have been able to afford the fees at Okeanos otherwise and he needed to row. The river kept him grounded and at peace.

A lapse in concentration cost him three grazed knuckles as the sandpaper slipped across his hand instead of the wood beneath it. He swore softly and sucked specks of blood off his skin before shaking away the pain.

"Enough."

The rough edge of the step was sanded smooth. Tiredly, he packed up everything he had been using, brushed an errant strand of hair from his eyes, then locked up. It was after ten and he had to be out of bed to open up at five-thirty. Even at this time of year, the early rowers would be arriving by six and Seb would have his hide if everything wasn't ready for them. The upside of the unsociable hours was that he could take a single scull out and have the river to himself for a while before anyone else got onto the water.

The boathouse flat was really little more than a bedsit, but Ben had made it as cozy as he could. His bed was covered with a warm patchwork quilt that was a little twee, but he felt that style could be sacrificed for comfort and warmth. Bright throws in autumnal colors covered the battered sofa and single armchair positioned in front of the wood burner. There was a small galley kitchen, and a desk and bookcase tucked into a corner. A tiny bathroom that didn't actually house a bath, just a temperamental shower, took up the only remaining space. He could always use the club facilities when it played up, though, so it didn't bother him too much.

Ben made a hot, milky cup of cocoa and spent a couple of hours working on an essay that was due in a few days. He was reading literature, and though the course didn't require many contact hours with his lecturers, the schedule of reading and written work was demanding. His tutor also had a reputation as an utter bastard who never gave extensions and was overly fond of his red pen—handing the essay in late just wouldn't be worth the aggravation. Ben didn't enjoy confrontation of any kind. His inherent need to please made him an effective peacekeeper and he had no wish to develop the kind of wild boy reputation that some of his peers seemed to delight in.

# More books from
# L.M. Somerton

*Love forged in fire is unassailable.*

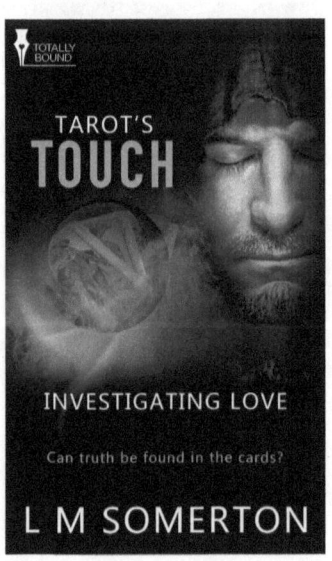

*Can truth be found in the cards?*

THE WYVERNS

RATTRAP

Sometimes the only way
to spring a trap is to
use live bait

L. M. SOMERTON

*Sometimes the only way to spring a trap is to use live bait.*

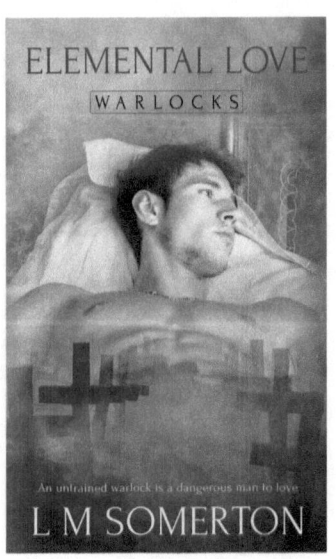

ELEMENTAL LOVE

WARLOCKS

An untrained warlock is a dangerous man to love

L M SOMERTON

*An untrained warlock is a dangerous man to love.*

# About the Author

**L.M. Somerton**

Lucinda lives in a small village in the English countryside, surrounded by rolling hills, cows and sheep. She started writing to fill time between jobs and is now firmly and unashamedly addicted.

She loves the English weather, especially the rain, and adores a thunderstorm. She loves good food, warm company and a crackling fire. She's fascinated by the psychology of relationships, especially between men, and her stories contain some subtle (and some not so subtle) leanings towards BDSM.

L.M. Somerton loves to hear from readers. You can find contact information, website details and an author profile page at https://www.pride-publishing.com/

PUBLISHING